M000012874

MONEY MAN

KING MAKER SERIES

TERRI E. LAINE

MONEY MAN

USA TODAY BESTSELLING AUTHOR

TERRI E. LAINE

Third Edition
Copyright 2023 Terri E. Laine

This is a work of fiction. Names, characters, places and incidents are
products of the author's imagination or are used factiously and are not to be
construed as real. Any resemblance to actual events, locales, organizations,
or persons living or dead, is entirely coincidental.
 All rights reserved. No part of this book may be used or reproduced in any
manner whatsoever without written permission, except in the case of brief
quotations embodied in critical articles or reviews. The scanning, uploading
and distribution of the book via the Internet or via any other means without
permission is illegal and punishable by law. Please purchase only authorized
electronic editions and do not participate in or encourage piracy of
copyrighted materials. Your support for the author's rights is appreciated.
For information address to SDTEL Books.

Michele @ Michele Catalano Creative - cover design
Sara Eirew - cover picture

AUTHOR'S 2ND NOTE

Many years ago, I wrote a story about Kalen and Bailey under a pen name I'd primarily used for young adult works. Though I'd hoped to be a crossover author as many at that time were, as a mother, I didn't think it right to promote such a romance with explicit themes that could be seen by younger reads. Thus the story failed in getting traction. I eventually took it off sale and it sat on my computer for years.

Present day. Now that I'd successfully written many novels under this new adult to adult author name, I thought why not dust Kalen and Bailey's story off and give it new life.

This started off as a project with light editing. I'd grown as a writer and I knew I would need to make minor changes.

However, as I got a few chapters in, my mind spun with ideas. And suddenly the story I'd written many years ago was no more. New and adjusted background stories for the main characters. A totally new spin on the plot and new twists. New dialogue and new chapters. As well as deleted dialogue, scenes and chapters. It just wasn't the same story.

If you were one of the few that read the original story, you may recognize the opening chapter, though even there have been several changes. But from there, things change drastically. Since it's no longer the same story and has a new trajectory, I won't mention the name of the old story.

Trust me when I say, it's different with vague similarities like the names of characters. Other than that, it's basically brand new.

Enjoy and Happy Reading!

PART
ONE

ONE

Pressed against the wall of a bathroom stall wasn't how I expected to spend New Year's Eve, especially with a stranger in front of me. Then again, he was the kind of gorgeous that would make any woman pant... like I was doing that very moment. But after all I'd been through in the past few weeks, I should have known better.

His husky groan brought me out of my head as he found the unnecessary garters under my skirt. The sound I made told a different story than my drunken brain was fooling me into believing. It was because of, not despite, recent events how I found myself here. I was one hundred percent smashed and on the verge of screwing a man I barely knew in the posh and seemingly clean bathroom in the exclusive club attached to the Eventi Hotel.

My body, a live wire, lit up as his electric fingers stroked purposefully between my inner thighs. What the hell was I doing? I wasn't this girl. Only two other people had ever known me this intimately. All the reasons why I shouldn't have dissolved as his lips trailed down my neck, nipping and making me squirm like a giggling teenager.

"Spread your legs," he commanded.

The deep timbre of his voice sported an accent my intoxicated brain couldn't make out. Though a picture of a sexy highlander from one of my historical romance novels popped in my head. What would it sound like if he called me lass?

A rumbling chuckle vibrated through him. "Lass, eh?"

Shit, had I said that out loud? And damn, it was as sexy as all get out to hear him call me that.

There was no time to think, as the tips of his fingers were about to make contact with my center in T-minus one. My body ignited like a rocket as he created pressure against my core. My thong provided no barrier as I grew wetter by the second. I should have been embarrassed, but his moves made me want to beg to be taken in ways I never had been before.

"You're dripping for me," he murmured a second before his lips were as soft as petals against my collarbone as he hungrily nibbled to the corner of my mouth, leaving behind the taste of expensive wine. The kind that had been passed around to all the guests of this evening's event. Including those on the dance floor in anticipation of the countdown. For the briefest of moments, I wondered where those crystal flutes had gone. We'd brought them with us when he led me here.

Those thoughts dissipated when he proficiently slid his hand up my shirt. Just as rapidly, he popped my right breast from the confines of my lacy bra in tandem with pushing a

2

finger, or possibly two, deep inside my slick depths. My eyes popped open. When had I closed them?

My need grew a thousand times higher as he sucked on one nipple. My gaze dropped and I noticed the two half-filled Waterford flutes at our feet before I slammed my head back into the tiled wall out of sheer pleasure. A gasp escaped my lips, and not from any head trauma. Pleasure won out over any stunned feelings from an incidental collision with the solid wall. Any reservations that hadn't been drowned by the alcohol flew out of my mind.

"Yes," I pleaded, needing more.

"Yes, what?" He growled like I was the honey to his hungry inner bear as his lips tasted my flesh.

My breast filled his mouth and his fingers continued to stroke in and out of me with precision. Then, as if he read my desire, his thumb skillfully brushed over my clit.

Overcome by the lightning building in my body, I said, "Fuck me."

Begging was the least of my concerns—my ego was no longer in play. A cry sailed out of my mouth as the first orgasm hit. He didn't stop and continued to stroke and rub, stroke and rub, prolonging my pleasure. As I crested the wave, my knees weakened. He responded by removing his fingers and cupping my ass one handed to steady me.

Damn, he was strong too. Total turn-on if I wasn't already. Then his free hand snapped the string of my thong, leaving it hanging but out of the way as I looked on.

"Now I'm going to fuck you," he stated as fact.

Still, that free hand wasn't done. He freed himself, tore open a condom with his teeth and slid the damn thing on with fluid movements. It happened so fast in the shadowy stall, I'd only heard the ripping of the foil.

It wouldn't be until later that I would consider how often he must have done this with other women, based on his skill level.

He pushed a big thigh between my legs to spread me wide, urging me to wrap them around his waist. Desire made me compliant and he lifted me off the ground and onto him. I didn't have time to think before he sheathed himself to the hilt deep inside me. I sucked in a breath, partly from pleasure and partly from pain, my eyes widening as he stretched me. I chastised myself for not looking at him first. He was clearly larger than anyone who'd been inside me before.

He froze in place and groaned. "Spread your legs wider. You're too fucking tight and I'm going to hurt you." I did as he asked, feeling him slide deeper as I did. "There, lass."

I sputtered, "I, I—" as he began to move in and out. The experience was like no other. All my nerve endings were on red alert as every stroke hit that magic button deep inside me. So much so I'd lost any ability to speak.

As the sensations grew, I tightened my legs around his waist, digging my heels in his back. I was shoved into a wall that wouldn't give, but it didn't matter. Especially not after I hit orgasms two and three before the faint Muzak in the background changed to the unmistakable midnight countdown.

Ten, his rhythm became erratic. *Nine*, he plunged in and out of me faster. *Eight*, he sucked hard on my pulse point, still pounding into me. There would be bruises. *Seven*, another orgasm quickly built inside of me with no

4

words to explain the how of it. *Six*, "fuck," he gritted out near my ear. *Five*, my fingers fisted in his hair, guiding his face to mine. *Four*, I bit him on the mouth, crazed by lust and desperation. *Three*, he pumped into me hard, my back taking a beating. *Two*, he sucked in my lower lip then took it between his teeth. *One*, he came, sending me into the wall with a final shove, pushing me over the edge one more time. A guttural sound so primitive left his mouth I had to see if he was still human.

Happy fucking New Year.

For the longest time, we remained molded like that. The heat we'd created cooled far too quickly as we remained locked together, my stilettos pinned to his back. Unfortunately for both of us, he eased out of me and I relaxed my leg lock, allowing him to slowly set me on my feet. My back slid down the wall before my four-inch heels hit the ground. Still, at my height of five feet five inches, I was much shorter than he.

"Aye, lass," he said, smirking, reminding me it had been my request for him to call me that. "Happy New Year," he finished, holding my gaze. His eyes were as green as the forest of Scottish lands, a place I'd longed to go. Staring into them, I could imagine myself there riding astride a horse with him chasing after me. I squeezed my thighs, sure I would combust by the sheer fantasy.

Only my brain chose that moment to come back online. Immediately, I was overcome by mortification at what I'd done. Good girls didn't have one-night stands with strangers. What would my mother think of me, not to mention my father who hadn't totally accepted that I'd left our community?

Unable to look at the stranger any longer, I closed my eyes, still caged by his massive arms, and smoothed down my skirt in the process.

"You like to scream, don't you, lass? Or was that just for me?"

I popped my eyes open as mortification stained my cheeks and caught sight of his smirk. Without a second thought, he picked up something from the ground—probably his wine glass—and left, not giving me a backwards glance.

Alone, I wondered ashamedly what I'd just done as a memory of my father's reprimanding glare formed in my head.

"Put your clothes on," he'd commanded after he'd sent Turner away.

Boys would be boys. I was the sinful Eve that had dangled the forbidden fruit.

He'd averted his eyes as I'd donned the neck-to-toe dress the women in our community were forced to wear.

"If I hadn't been the one to catch you, you'd be branded, or worse, excommunicated." Disgust filled my father's voice.

I felt one foot tall. I might not have liked the rules where women were considered little more than breeding stock, but I didn't want him looking at me like I was one of those worldly women we were warned about.

"The shame you've caused our family and put on your sisters if he tells his father."

I hadn't thought about my sisters. They would be branded for my sins and would be lucky to be chosen as sister wives if the truth came out.

"He won't. He loves me," I pleaded.

"You better hope they will consider a wedding."

Then my father had turned, dismissing me much like the stranger had. It didn't matter that I hadn't married or that my mother had gotten me out. I still felt that scarlet S burning in my chest and I ran out of the bathroom. I wanted to put as much distance between me and my sins as I could.

How could I have let him have me after only knowing him—how long? Minutes, an hour tops, maybe?

I was desperate to leave and needed to find the friend I'd come with—rather my best friend—the one who hadn't stopped me from making this colossal fuck-up.

TWO

Shoving open the restroom door, I realized just how soundproof the bathroom had been. With it open, the noise from the party hit me like I'd face-planted into a wall. I nearly stumbled back, but my determination to get away pushed me forward. Unsteady on my feet due to the alcohol —or because I had been thoroughly fucked, I kept going.

One thing I was grateful for was that we'd been the only occupants of the place as far as I could tell in my hasty retreat. That was probably because it had been so close to midnight.

Winding my way through the masses of people on the dance floor, I eventually found my way back to Lizzy. She was exactly where I had left her, glued to the guy who had found her the same time my stranger had found me.

Briefly, I'd wondered if the two guys were friends, because they'd approached us from behind at the same time. Lizzy and I had been drunk dancing together, giving anyone close a show.

I'd only gotten a passing glance at the guy who'd occupied her time before I tuned into my own sex-on-two-legs. Now getting a better look, her guy was very attractive and just a bit taller than her with a crown of dark blond hair and sexy scruff.

Apparently, during my time away, the pair was heading down the same path I'd been on. Lip-locked like long-lost lovers, they were grinding into each other like they needed a room. But, who was I to judge? I'd found a room in the form of a bathroom stall.

I hated to interrupt, but this was an emergency because on top of feeling like a whore, I also had to deal with the stranger's rejection. I was probably his worst fuck ever. Exactly what Scott had told me as his reason he'd cheated on me. I could barely hold back the sickness in my gut. I had to leave before I completely lost it.

I tapped frantically on Lizzy's back and she slowly disengaged herself from her man who had to be a super-model. Who knew there were so many hot single guys in New York? He was gorgeous. *And what was I thinking?* Like a whore apparently.

Lizzy's eyes narrowed on me. I knew that stare. She wasn't pleased I'd cut in.

"Look, I have to get out of here. Either you're coming with or I'll see you later," I said, standing on my toes to reach her ear.

Lizzy was taller than me by several inches, even in the heels I wore.

"What?" she said, holding out her hands in surrender, searching my eyes for an explanation.

"Later," I said, turning away, suddenly feeling like I had seconds before I became violently ill from all the alcohol as memories of the past and of my present situation collided in my head. I needed to get away. I needed air. I heard her call out my name as I ran.

Outside, the crisp air hit me like the frost that escaped my mouth, instant and telling. Light puffy flakes flurried in the air as I hurried to the curb with my arm outstretched, hoping against hope for a cab at this hour on this night in New York City. I berated myself for not getting the Uber app like Lizzy had suggested. Thankfully, we weren't in Times Square. Tears spilled from my eyes as I stared at the dirty curb, wanting to fall to my knees but thinking better of it. This night might just go down in history as one of my biggest regrets.

An arm came over my shoulder and I snapped around to see who it was. I sighed in relief when I spotted Lizzy. She held out my coat for me to shrug into. Damn, that was why I was so cold.

I could see the questions in her eyes. Why was I acting like a lunatic? And her answer if she'd known what I'd done. It wasn't like I was the first girl to have a one-night stand, right? She'd say before adding who would blame me for it after all that had happened?

"What the hell, Bails?" Lizzy said as I slipped into the wool.

That's when it hit me. *Bile* like a geyser ready to erupt. That fifth fruity drink had been too much. A yellow cab just pulled up from my earlier hail when I tossed my cookies onto the very curb I'd contemplated sitting on. It splashed as it left my mouth and landed on the ground. God knew what else besides vomit spattered onto Lizzy's and my shoes. My friend's Jimmy Choos might be ruined, but she held my hair like only a good bestie would.

"Yous two getting in or what?" came a voice from the open window of the cab.

The cabbie didn't seem bothered that I was choking out the entire contents of my stomach. After a final retch, Lizzy opened the door and helped me inside. As our ride pulled away, I made the mistake of looking back.

Part of me hoped that the best sex of my life had come for me. As if fate granted me a gift, my first for the new year, Mr. Tall, Hard, and Fuck Me walked out of the hotel. I shimmied down in my seat before his gaze could possibly lock onto mine.

The drive shouldn't have been long, but with Times Square attendees finding other places to go, the streets were packed. The ride was awful for my still rebelling stomach. With every bump and turn, I battled not to puke.

Once home, Lizzy made me a cup of ginger tea and I warmed my hands around the mug. The blanket wrapped around me was added comfort while I sat in a chair next to the gas fireplace and stared absently at my friend.

"So, tell me, why did we have to leave that amazing party?" she asked with her fist underneath her chin. I was grateful she didn't seem pissed.

I had to give her bonus points for not pressing me on the ride home and waiting until I'd showered like someone needing cleansing from potential radiation poisoning, changed, and brushed my teeth before finally asking me what the hell my problem was, in such a nice-Lizzy way.

"I had sex in the bathroom," I blurted, though I knew how this conversation would play out.

Perched directly across from me, Lizzy didn't react right away. Her legs hung lazily over the side of one arm. Eyes wide, she leaned forward as if she were about to tell a secret. "With the guy from the dance floor you left with?"

I nodded as the weight of my actions tightened my chest.

"Holy shit, Bails. Was it good? Did you come?"

Leave it to my best friend to want details.

"That isn't the point," I cried, feeling the bite of tears at my slut-shaming choice. "I had sex with a guy I don't even know."

Rolling her eyes and waving her hand, she said, "Bails, you deserve a good shag. Just tell me. Was it great or what?"

Unable to lie to my best friend, I paused. How had it been? I'd been so filled with regret, I hadn't given that question any consideration until now.

"It was phenomenal," I whispered, the confession falling off my tongue as I admitted it not only to her but to myself.

"Then what the fuck?" she said. "No pun intended." She chuckled to herself as I got more irritated by the second. I started to push to my feet.

Lizzy had no idea of the baggage I carried. The rules of behavior that had been beaten into me hadn't disappeared after I'd left the community. They'd played a role in every decision I made even after the fact.

"Wait, Bails. I'm sorry. It's just you're all worked up over nothing. You deserve this. After everything that asshole, Scott, put you through. I bet he never made you come in the three years you two were together."

The mention of Scott should have brought tears to my

eyes. I'd loved him, hadn't I? Yet I was numb. Maybe I never loved him? Or had I stayed in that relationship because of my upbringing?

Then Lizzy's words came back to me. Curiosity won over my conscience for a second. Had Scott ever made me come? The question should be ridiculous. We'd been together so long. Our sex life had been fine. Hadn't it? Maybe I was still too drunk because I was fuzzy on the details.

Only thinking about sex brought me back to my encounter with the stranger, who remained nameless, a reminder that a scarlet A should be embroidered on my chest, or rather an S for slut.

What the hell had I done?

It had started on the dance floor, the way he sparked fantasies in me. His body fit perfectly with mine despite his height. The way he moved against me I'd been driven into lust. He'd barely had to touch me to set me ablaze. The line of fire he created headed directly to my core. And when the explosion melted me down, he must have seen it. Desire had burned bright in his eyes too.

When he'd begun to lead me from the dance floor, I'd gone willingly with the promise of more to come. And I had come, three, maybe four times. Scott had never made me have multiple orgasms. That much I was sure of.

"Bails..." From a distance, I thought I heard my name. "Bailey!" Lizzy's near shouting brought me out of my internal thoughts and I stopped twisting the braided ring on my right hand that I hadn't ever taken off. She didn't often say my whole name, so I lifted my head, feeling a blush cross my cheeks. A sly grin played on her mouth. "Tell me all now, or I'll kick you out of my house," she declared teasingly.

I had nowhere else to go, not just yet at least. And though she'd said the words, she would never kick me out. Still, I spilled every detail to her, needing to get it out. Maybe then the burden could leave my chest. It wasn't like I was ever going to see the man again.

"That's fucking hot," Lizzy said. "From what I saw of him, he was gorg."

He had been undeniably gorgeous. Women had stared at me with envy, bolstering my steps toward the abyss of sin.

"Hot or not, I hope to never see him again," I admitted, heat still burning in my cheeks.

She may be my best friend, but I wasn't one to kiss and tell, especially with details of sex. The one and only time I'd told her about Scott and me, it had been our first time together. After hearing the tale, she had immediately declared it was boring and hadn't asked much about our doings thereafter.

Lizzy pursed her lips in that way of hers. "Bails, you have nothing to be ashamed of. You didn't shag him alone."

Though her words were true, it wasn't how I'd been brought up. She didn't know the full story about the separatist community I'd grown up in. Our lives were governed based on traditional religious views where women were expected to be as pure as the first fallen snow. There had been no such thing as sex before marriage. Without the use of technology, we had no visuals that life could be any different. Lizzy could never fully understand the life I'd escaped.

Again I rubbed over the ring that was a source of

comfort and of pain. It was a symbol of the past I hadn't yet been fully able to let go.

"He probably thinks I'm some slut." There was that word again. I hid my face behind a curtain of my hands. And damn my childhood that I worried more about how a man saw me above my own feelings.

"Who cares? You had a great fuck on what would have been your wedding night. You basically screwed Scott by fucking that guy."

My wedding night. I was reminded it would have been tonight if I hadn't left Scott a few weeks ago.

She laughed at her own joke, breaking into my thoughts. It might have been funny if we were talking about someone else. But this was me. And I wasn't that girl, or I shouldn't be.

"I'm going to bed," I said, rising from my seat. I just needed to sleep it off.

Being a good friend, Lizzy knew when to lay off. "Night, Bails. And don't forget your date tomorrow with the guy my mom set you up with."

Groaning, I rolled my eyes. The last thing I wanted to do was go on a date. Seeing my annoyance, she giggled again. I headed to the bedroom that had been temporarily turned into mine—at least until I found somewhere else to live since Scott had moved into our would be home with the woman he'd cheated on me with.

THREE

KALEN

My fingers brushed over the scrap of silk I'd shoved into my pocket when I'd left the loo as I reached for cash to close out my tab. That had been an impulse move that puzzled me now. I didn't need a reminder of the redhead.

Yet an image of her head thrown back filled my mind. As my cock began to harden, I quickly dismissed it. She'd been a distraction, nothing more.

"Bro."

The word shattered my thoughts as a solid hand landed on my back and I turned to face the voice.

"Connor," I acknowledged just as a leggy blonde and a curvy brunette swaggered up on either side of him.

"You aren't leaving?" he asked with a raised brow and glanced over at his company one at a time.

The women on his arm giggled and one pointed, letting her hungry gaze drop to my cock as if she could see through my pants.

"I am," I said.

The women were attractive but looked more like they could be bought like the scotch I'd had earlier. I didn't pay for sex. Not that Conner did, but he wasn't as choosy about his bed partners as I was.

"Another scotch and I want to close out my tab," I told the bartender. Points to him for nodding and not asking me to repeat myself as so many Americans did.

Thankfully, when I turned Connor was alone. Apparently, the women took the hint and left. "I brought you here tonight to have some fucking fun, not be a wanker."

His American accent didn't fit with the British word, but I ignored him.

He shifted to stand next to me at the counter. "Pussy's got your tongue?" he quipped.

His choice of words to replace "cat" only made me glare at him. He knew me well enough to hold his hands up in surrender.

"It's just I saw you with a hot redhead earlier. Did you scare her off?"

"Didn't you have company?" I asked dryly, not answering his question.

"I did. One for me and one for you. But you scared them off too."

I turned away from his probing glare as the bartender appeared with the Lagavulin and poured me another two fingers. I tossed it back before putting down a couple of fifties. I left them next to my empty glass and met Connor's quizzical gaze.

"I'm headed home," I announced, having already made the decision to call it a night.

I caught sight of the blonde the redhead was with

earlier making a dash for the door. I looked back at my brother.

Connor's lips had thinned. "You're going to be old before your time," he said, pointing at me.

"Some of us have work in the morning," I said, getting to my feet.

"I work," he said with a grin showing all his teeth.

"You play," I said. "Not all of us have that privilege."

His smile was never ending as I turned my back on him. He didn't follow as I made my way out after notifying my driver.

I stepped out into the night, greeted by blowing snowflakes, a reminder of home and all I'd left behind. If I wanted to conquer an empire, there were deals to be made. Negotiations for one in particular began tomorrow. I smiled to myself, thinking about that one. I had a feeling that deal wouldn't be sealed in a conference room.

FOUR

BAILEY

I OPENED MY EYES, BUT QUICKLY CLOSED THEM AGAINST the brightness of the sunlight filtering into the room. Waking up hungover was never fun. And for me, it wasn't a regular occurrence. Though I recognized the symptoms.

Even though I'd thrown up most of what I'd consumed the night before on the curb, enough alcohol had been absorbed in my bloodstream for my head to pound like a marching band paraded through it.

Slipping my feet over the side of the bed took considerable effort. Once standing, I got the most uncomfortable sensation between my thighs. Yes, I had most definitely been banged hard last night—as if I needed the reminder. I ached at my very center. On wobbly feet, I headed to my private bath, courtesy of Lizzy's kindness.

Finding an apartment in New York on short notice was an impossibility. Thankfully, my former college roommate had an empty room she eagerly lent to me at no charge and no restrictions on the length of my stay. Still, I was on the hunt for a place of my own because I didn't want to take advantage of her kindness, even if she didn't need money.

Looking in the mirror, I pushed back the auburn mass of my hair to spill down my back. Today, it looked redder than usual. I wasn't sure if that was because of my mood or if it was because it was winter. Summer seemed to bring out more of my natural highlights.

After washing my face and brushing my teeth, my pale blue eyes stared blankly back at me in the mirror. They looked familiar, yet I wasn't sure about the woman who reflected in the mirror.

Who was I? What had I done with Bailey Glicks, the girl who'd grown up believing people should save themselves for marriage? Sex had been taboo. Hell, sex after marriage was meant for procreation, not pleasure.

I often wondered if maybe I'd left home a little over four years ago for sexual freedom over the possibility of a career outside of the home or maybe it was both. If my parents knew just how far from grace I'd fallen, would my father ever allow me home to see my mom or siblings again?

I shoved those thoughts away and tried to believe that Lizzy was right. What was done was done. I couldn't take it back. If I was honest with myself, I'd enjoyed it—a lot. I'd never felt that way before, free and acting on my own instinct instead of the will of others.

In the kitchen, I pulled out a bottle of Perrier because Lizzy didn't have regular bottled water. I couldn't fault her. She'd been brought up with a diamond-encrusted spoon in her mouth. My parents wouldn't understand or approve of all the modern conveniences that were right at home in this kitchen, especially the stainless-steel appliances that hadn't seen much use until I came along. Marble countertops finished off the place, and on top of them sat a crystal Waterford bowl that before I'd arrived had only been decoration. Because of me, it now had a purpose holding fruit. I grabbed a banana and started to peel it. I still felt sick, but bananas were rumored to help ease the effects of a hangover.

Sitting at the counter, I dreaded going over to Lizzy's parents' house for New Year's brunch. Then later, I had a date with a stockbroker. Yay for me... not.

"Morning, sex goddess," Lizzy teased, striding into the kitchen, looking flawless as always.

"Bite me," I said back. I was a morning person, unlike Lizzy, but today for good reason I was very grumpy.

She popped her flavor selection into her fancy coffee maker and turned back to me. "So, how is your conscience this morning?"

I so didn't need the reminder of last night.

"The same, bruised and on the verge of death," I answered flatly. She giggled, thinking I was making a joke, when I was being dead serious. Then I turned the tides on her. "I didn't ask you about the guy whose tongue you swallowed while bringing in the new year. Did you get his name and business card?" The last bit was a dig because Lizzy didn't normally date guys who had business cards or could even spell "business card." She liked them rough around the edges.

"Yes, that sexy man was Hans. He's an up-and-coming model from Sweden."

"I knew it. I'd pegged him for a model." He had been too tall and too pretty to be anything else, from what I remembered. "I'm sure your mother would approve," I said, cheekily winking at her, wanting to forget my choices.

"It wouldn't be her first choice. But she'd probably be happier with him than any other guy I've dated. Besides, she's not going to find out. I'm just glad you moved here so she can force dates onto you instead of me."

I sighed as she laughed. My showing up on Lizzy's door the week before Christmas with my story of betrayal by my fiancé had definitely taken some of the *being single* heat off of her. Her mother, Kathryn, had expected her to go to school to find a husband. A degree was a side benefit.

"We're going to be late," Lizzy said, winking as she drank her coffee. I knew that being late was a pet peeve of her mother's, so I nodded and headed to my room to get ready for brunch.

By the time we made it the few blocks over to Lizzy's parents' place, my hangover was almost a thing of the past. The banana and water had helped significantly, so I was able to walk without pain showing on my face. I wasn't a good actress and Kathryn had a discerning eye.

Inside their home, which was a lavish two-floor Park Avenue apartment within walking distance of Central Park, I was welcomed with two quick kisses on either side of my face by both of her parents. Her tall, regal father, Ted, was still an extremely handsome man with a full head of gray. Her mother stood at five feet nine—as tall as her daughter— and was still a blonde through and through, natural or not. Not a question I would ever ask.

We walked into her receiving room, which was deco- rated with a gray settee and two matching gray flowered patterned chairs, and sat while a butler brought in tea and coffee.

I took a seat near Lizzy in one of the dainty chairs while her parents sat on the settee opposite us. While we waited to be served, Kathryn asked, "How was your evening, dear?"

Lizzy turned and winked at me. I wanted to scowl at her but kept the smile on my face. "Fine, great even." I was surprised at how easily that lie had come. There was no way I'd explain how my night really went as a blush blossomed on my face. The lie I told wouldn't hold if I couldn't keep a straight face.

"Good, good," Kathryn said. "And you, Lizzy dear, how are you today?"

Lizzy, looking elegant and every bit like she belonged in this world, said, "Well, a bit tired if I must say."

My smile slipped as my decorum faltered. My legs were crossed, but my hands, which were in my lap—ladylike, just how Kathryn had taught me—wanted to fist. Lizzy was playing games, like she planned to out me.

Thankfully, the butler walked in and announced, "Brunch is served."

Ted stood, holding out a hand to his wife and helping her to her feet. "Well, I'm sorry to hear of it. I guess we'll keep brunch short so you can return home and lie down."

Behind her parents' back, I pinched my wayward best friend, who only giggled. But I had to give it to her. She'd given us cause to leave if we wanted to.

We were ushered into the formal dining room, which held a king's table, or rather a table that was far too large for two people. Four high-backed chairs were placed around the table, two at the head and foot and the other two opposite each other, exactly midway on the long end.

The pristine white-rimmed silver china was already set. Her mother currently had a thing for silver. The flatware was perfectly set for each course. Everything always in its place here, just as Kathryn wanted it to be.

Being Lizzy's best friend all through college, I'd been semi-adopted by her family when mine was seemingly absent from my life and I'd been coached on all proper etiquette for a young lady.

Her parents sat across from each other at the far ends of the table, which in this case didn't actually mean what the subtext suggested. They did, in fact, get along. Lizzy and I sat across from each other in close proximity.

The butler from earlier didn't make an appearance. Instead, he orchestrated the wait staff, which appeared shortly after we'd settled, brought in the first course, and brunch began. Ted brought us up to date with current events, from politics to the weather, while the first course was removed.

It was always good to get his updates because I didn't watch much news or read the paper regularly. It was simply too depressing. And up until this summer, I had been all about graduating with my degree in accounting, after which my efforts were focused on studying for the CPA exam.

Pleasant conversation continued throughout the meal. I was happy the subject of my love life hadn't come up. By the time dessert was served, I was well-versed in all the hot-button topics of the day.

"Ted, is it true what they are saying about King?" Kathryn asked her husband.

I perked up as the name King was huge in New York.

He shrugged. "Now that he's got that nasty diagnosis, it's rumored his son has taken over."

"I hear they call his son the Money Man," Lizzy said and winked at me.

Kathryn scowled at her daughter. "Stop. That sounds like one of those rapper names."

Lizzy shrugged. "I heard he's hot and making crazy money for investors."

"And catching the eye of the SEC," Ted countered.

The SEC was a branch of the government that oversaw the financial markets to protect investors.

Though I considered Lizzy's family my own, I kept my lips shut that I would be a part of the team auditing that company on Monday. I hadn't known until then why we'd been called in when our firm wasn't their primary auditors. But what Lizzy said made me curious.

"I wonder if he's as hot as rumors say," Lizzy mused.

I wasn't as plugged in as everyone around the table. Yet it surprised me that someone so seemingly powerful hadn't been captured in any pictures. "You haven't seen him?" I asked no one in particular.

"Mom?" Lizzy asked, directing my question to her.

"My understanding is that he went to boarding school once his mother left," she answered.

People had phones. These days you couldn't sneeze on the streets of New York without fear you'd become a meme.

"There are no pictures of him?" I asked.

Kathryn shrugged. "I've seen some with him as a boy at Royce King's home. But it's been years."

Ted added, "Once we moved our funds from his company, we haven't exactly been invited over."

"Maybe I should date one of the King boys," Lizzy said, taunting her mother, who looked almost ready to choke.

There were multiple boys? "There are two?" I mouthed to Lizzy and she nodded.

It was easy to see the Kings had fallen out of favor with high society, at least in her parents' eyes.

"Are you ready for your date tonight?" Kathryn asked, effectively changing the subject.

And to think I'd almost gotten off unscathed. I ignored the smirk on Lizzy's face and said, "Yes, I'm looking forward to it." Not! I kicked Lizzy lightly under the table. It didn't stop her quiet laughter.

Really, I was so not looking forward to this. In fact, I pitied this guy. Whoever he was, he wouldn't get a fair shot. I just wasn't in the mood for a date. After last night, I just wanted some me time and, truth be told, I was more curious than ever about the King family.

I would be starting my new work assignment tomorrow and maybe I'd run into one of the Kings. Some extra sleep would serve me better. On top of that, who goes on a blind date on New Year's Day? I wasn't sure why I had agreed to it. But apparently, the stockbroker, also fairly new at his job, rarely had a day off.

"He's a good boy. He's a Wilshire of the Park Avenue Wilshires. You'd do well marrying into that family."

Marriage? I wasn't ready to date, let alone marry. But Kathryn had set this up. There was no turning back. And honestly, after all they'd done for me, how could I possibly say no? Still, I'd heard this all before. First, these *dates* had been directed at Lizzy, until her mother had finally given up. Lizzy didn't care if she made a spectacle of herself and pissed off some guy who wasn't her type. She didn't care about the ramifications to her family's reputation.

Not long after, Lizzy threatened that she was going to faint and got us out of there before her mother started planning a wedding for the stockbroker and me. By the time we made it back to her place, I was mentally exhausted.

"What are you going to wear?" Lizzy questioned with an arched eyebrow.

She was draped over her white furniture as usual in such a casual way I wondered just how it stayed so pristine.

"Can't I just cancel?" I groaned, considering blowing the guy off for the millionth time.

It wasn't like we'd ever met. Who could blame me? I'd just broken up with my fiancé a few short weeks ago.

Lizzy shook her head. "Not unless you want to explain it to my mother."

Sighing, I headed to my room, directly to the closet. If I'd cared about meeting a Wilshire from the Park Avenue Wilshires, I might have borrowed something from Lizzy to wear. Still, I couldn't make a bad impression and embarrass her family.

And no, I didn't want to think about last night. Yet I was doing it anyway, my thoughts scattering. I had to get back to the matter at hand—a date had been made and needed to be kept, saving my best friend the trouble.

I put on a black pencil skirt, an emerald shirt that worked well with my hair color, and black heels and hoped he wasn't short.

The doorman called to let us know my visitor was on his

way up according to Lizzy, who'd popped into the bathroom to inspect me.

"You look good," she said.

"Crap," I said. "Maybe I should wear a sack."

She laughed. "Give the poor guy a chance. He could be the one."

"I'm not ready for the one," I complained, yet I laughed along with her. She left to answer the door and entertain him while I finished up.

When I stepped into the living room, my bestie was flirting with my date, something she did well. After I got a glimpse of a cute guy with a dimple, I could see why. Maybe this evening wouldn't be so bad after all.

FIVE

A car waited for us at the curb, and I was already impressed with the guy. He was a couple inches taller than me in heels. *Check*. His sandy brown hair was fashionably cut, not too short and not too long. He was easy on the eyes. *Check*.

If only I felt good about being out with a guy. I most certainly had fallen far from grace. Sleeping with a stranger one night and on a date with another the next all while knowing I'd been set to marry mere weeks ago. My father was right about me.

"I hope you don't mind. I made reservations at the 21 Club," he said, shattering my thoughts.

"Sounds good," I replied, though I looked out the window trying too hard not to sound uninterested. He seemed nice and didn't deserve my lack of enthusiasm. I touched my ring, grounding myself into the present.

He prattled on about how lucky he'd been to get the reservation. I'd only heard about the place and knew he wasn't scrimping on our date.

"You look beautiful, by the way," he added, giving me a dimpled grin.

I forced a smile, wanting to enjoy tonight somehow.

"Thanks," I said and managed to add, "You too."

We walked into the main level of the restaurant, but were quickly led upstairs to a more intimate, romantic setting. Several tables were filled with guests quietly enjoying their meals. My date held my chair out for me— the guy was racking up points faster than I could count.

Everything so far was perfect. Or maybe my low expectations fueled the good feelings.

We were discussing the menu selections when the unthinkable happened. After a second glance, I was pretty sure my first and only one-night stand walked in with a tall, beautiful brunette on his arm. Involuntarily, I lifted my menu to hide my face as color filled my cheeks.

Although I couldn't see my date, I heard the frown in his voice when he asked, "Are you okay?"

"Yes," I said, probably looking like a small child as I peered around the menu.

I needed to get it together. The stockbroker wasn't stupid. He turned around, looking for who or what I may have seen. Thankfully, Mr. Fuck Me hadn't once looked in my direction, seemingly focused on the woman across from him.

Although I was still partially hidden, my date was polite enough not to ask again. To ease some of the awkwardness, I peppered him with questions about what to choose for an entrée, giving me cause for my position behind the menu. Hopefully to him, I appeared to be studying the options instead of masking my face behind a barrier.

Dumbly, I realized I would have to put my menu down before the waiter approached to take our order. Reluctantly, I did. My one-night stand continued not to notice me, and after a while I relaxed into conversation.

Retrospectively, it had been dark last night and we'd both been drinking. *Maybe my one-time mistake didn't remember me*, or so I told myself. He obviously didn't have problems getting women.

While the stockbroker talked about his job at my prompting, I found myself periodically gazing at the guy who'd had me begging him to fuck me the night before. No longer in a darkened ballroom or shrouded bathroom, I could see for sure he was as devastatingly gorgeous as I remembered. And I wasn't the only one to notice. Other women in the room, young and old alike, couldn't keep their eyes off him. His thick black hair, strong profile sculpted from all things pleasing, and mouth that promised all kinds of sensual pleasures were alluring. I could barely keep my eyes off him.

"Bailey," my date said, capturing my attention.

I turned quickly to him. "Yes," I replied, blinking rapidly, knowing I'd been caught.

"I'm told you're a CPA for a big international firm," he repeated.

"Oh," I replied, feeling guilty that I hadn't been paying any attention to him. It was rude. "I'm just a first-year auditor, not really as exciting as your job."

"I think you would make anything interesting," he said, focused solely on me.

Gratefully, the first course showed up and I didn't have to respond. As much as I didn't want to notice the other man, the nameless guy had captured all my attention. I found myself inappropriately damp at the sight of him.

Then again, my body remembered. So much so, I kept stealing looks in his direction. He made taking a drink an incredibly erotic experience, which was crazy.

Somehow, I'd managed to keep up with the dinner conversation while honing my stalker abilities. By the time the empty entrée plates were removed from my table, I had to excuse myself to go to the ladies' room. I needed to freshen up, and badly. Mr. Fuck Me ate his food in a way that reminded me how he'd nibbled on me.

I skirted by his table without him looking up at me. In the bathroom, I took care of cleanup. Then I stared at myself long and hard in the mirror.

I could hear my father chastising me. *Just shameful*, he would chide and for more reasons than because I couldn't keep my eyes off the man who wasn't even my date.

Forget about him, I told myself. The proper thing to do was to concentrate on the guy who had taken me out for the night. *Yeah right, easier said than done*, I thought.

After reapplying lip gloss, I headed out the door and right into a wall.

"Excuse me," I said before looking up. And up. There he was.

"Bailey," he said in a heavily accented and extremely sexy voice. My clear brain recognized the Scottish brogue I'd missed before.

Shocked, I sniped, "How do you know my name?"

He stared at me with an unreadable expression. "A guess. Your friend called it out as she ran after you," he said matter-of-factly.

He'd flustered me with his closeness, stirring my arousal.

"I didn't run away," I lied, and not convincingly.

He shrugged. "I'll leave you to your date."

The fact that he seemed not to care one way or the other embarrassed me more.

"And back to yours," I snapped, sounding petty and jealous as he moved to leave.

"Jealous," he said, with an arching brow.

Clearing my throat, I felt the need to set the record straight. "No," I said emphatically and belatedly added, "Besides, last night shouldn't have happened. I'm not that kind of woman."

"And here I thought this was an invitation."

"An invitation," I said incredulously. My blood boiled and not for the reasons it had moments before.

"Yes, considering your penchant for bathroom stalls." A smirk appeared on his beautiful face. "Or maybe you're wet, remembering how I fucked you last night."

Of all the—as I dug for a snarky response, somehow the distance between us closed, leaving only a sliver of space. Desire ratcheted up in me, but also unnerving me.

"Are you wet for me, lass?" he asked, confidence radiating in his cold gaze.

"What?—Wait?—No! You're on a date with another woman."

And that was the biggest lie ever.

He didn't hesitate with his answer. "Dinnae concern yourself with her."

"Concern," I said, sounding way too breathy instead of

angry. "I'm not concerned. Just curious why you're here with me," I challenged.

I wanted to take the words back as quickly as I'd said them. Before I had the chance, he answered.

"I could ask the same?" His brow lifted.

People were passing us in the narrow hallway, mostly servers, and he hadn't given them a single glance. He continued to cage me as if we were alone.

"Does your little boyfriend know what you did with me last night?"

"Little?" I asked as if that was the most important part of what he'd asked.

"He looks barely older than a teenager."

The stockbroker did have a baby face, but I wasn't about to agree with him.

"Last night was a mistake. And even though it's none of your business, he's not my boyfriend. He's my date and none of your concern." I put emphasis on the last word, reminding him of his.

"Yet you're here with me, not him," he said, repeating my statement from earlier.

He was too confident, leaving me off balance until his eyes shifted to the bathroom door. That snapped some sense into me. I shoved down my shame and instead reached for anger.

"Fuck you," I said.

For me it was a declaration of war. Words I didn't use often and should have been the verbal slap I'd meant them to be.

"I already have, lass, and I freely admit I love to fuck.

And from the sounds you made last night, you do too. The question is, where will we fuck next?"

His smug grin told me he fully expected we'd do it right now.

His arrogance should have been a total turn-off. Yet I still wanted him, which confused the mess out of me when reminded of my damnable actions the night before.

Turning from his green-eyed stare, I glanced over his shoulder before speaking. "Never going to happen. Now, if you'll excuse me, I need to get back," I said way too quickly, unable to keep it together in his presence.

He stepped closer, which didn't seem possible, and his hand landed on my thigh.

"You're only lying to yourself." The words rumbled from low in his throat and sent a shiver of excitement through me. Especially as his fingers pushed higher, burning me with lust. My center clenched, and I swore if he touched my core, I would spontaneously combust.

"I have to go," I sputtered, completely unsure of myself. I'd never been in a situation like this before.

"Then why aren't you leaving?" His breath fanned across my ear.

The sexual tension between us was undeniable, but my date waited for me. "I am."

He pulled back just enough to take his warmth with him, and unfortunately for me I missed it instantly.

"So go." He held out a hand as if to direct my path.

I hesitated long enough for victory to fill his expression.

"Just like I thought. You want me," he stated as fact.

His confidence was like a wet blanket snapping me out of the lustful haze.

"Ego much?" I snapped.

"Tell me you don't," he dared.

I tried to force the lie from my mouth, but he beat me to it.

"Wear a skirt tomorrow and don't bother with underwear," he demanded.

I was too startled by his statement to offer any objection as a war between desire and common sense waged within me. This cocky jerk-face of a man was dangerous to my self-preservation. What he wanted was clear, and it wasn't really me. Wanting him was just as foolish on so many levels and wasn't what my mending broken heart needed.

"I don't even know your name," I said, injecting as much haughtiness as I could.

Then I waited for an answer as if I was considering his offer. I should have been walking away with my head held high and never looking back. I was aware I'd been gone far too long from my date to be considered polite. I'd been taught better.

His eyes searched mine several beats before he answered. "Kalen."

He continued to watch me as if waiting for some sort of reaction. Was he lying to me about his name?

"Kalen," I repeated.

The space between us evaporated, leaving not a breath there. "I want to hear you say that when my cock is buried deep inside you."

My heart raced as his hand gripped my waist and gave it a squeeze.

"I have to go," I said in a lame attempt to leave when my feet were glued to the ground.

"Tomorrow," he commanded.

His conceit cleared my head some.

"I don't think so," I said with more self-assuredness than I felt.

He brought his mouth so close to mine, I forgot all about his demanding tone. Instead, my memory flashed back to what he'd done to me with it the previous night. I squeezed my legs together as if I could stop the need gathering there.

"Eight o'clock," he declared as if it were a forgone conclusion that I'd be there. Then he took a step back, and smirked. "Or not."

Damn him, the arrogant ass. He looked as though he didn't care either way as "lass" rolled off his tongue in an invitation I found hard to deny. Free, I moved, but caught his parting words as I glanced over my shoulder.

"Your choice."

I stared into those lush green eyes before I fled back into the dining room. Dessert had been served and my date waited patiently for me. I took a few cleansing breaths before I got to the table. The arrogant Kalen had acted as though I was his, and some unfamiliar part of me wanted it.

When I sat, my date looked happy to see me. I felt like such a bad person. There I was, lusting over an asshat while on a date with a guy who was actually really nice.

"Sorry," I said, and tried not to glance over at Kalen.

He was focused on his date once again, not paying attention to me at all like before. Yet he hadn't been surprised to run into me out in the hallway. It was as if he'd been waiting for me.

Taking a page out of the ass' playbook, I focused back

on my date, praying that I wouldn't ruin the rest of the night.

I tried for light conversation, and I failed. The poor guy kept repeating his questions to me because I couldn't focus on him. My attention kept diverting to Kalen and his unwavering gaze on the woman with him. Why was that a turn-on?

My date was about to give me a taste of his chocolate cake with pears and cranberry sorbet when a clatter had everyone looking around. One of the servers dropped some silverware while clearing a nearby table.

As I looked up, I caught Kalen's humorous gaze. That's when I noticed the stockbroker's hand covering mine.

Unable to stop myself, I pulled my hand free and pushed my hair back in order to temper my date's confused expression.

Why was I letting that man get to me? I placed my hands in my lap and smiled at the guy across the table from me.

Soon after dessert was gone and the bill paid, we stood to leave. My stockbroker helped me out of my chair. Since Kalen was still seated, there was no way around passing by him. I felt my date's hand touch my lower back in a gentlemanly way to guide me out of the room. Kalen stood just as we neared, wedging himself between us.

"Sorry," he said. His accent was utterly sexy and totally unremorseful. I turned back in time for Kalen to bend down quickly and whisper to me, "Sweet dreams."

Open-mouthed, I watched my one-night stand not miss a beat to help his *date* out of her chair. I quickly turned away and moved at a respectable pace just out of reach.

Damn him.

SIX

LIZZY LOUNGED ON HER CHAIR AS I ENTERED THE apartment.

"How'd it go?" she asked with a smirk on her face.

I dropped to the couch and sighed.

"It was going well until Kalen."

"Kalen?" she asked.

"He's the guy—"

"The guy," she said with wide eyes. "From last night?"

I nodded and told her the story.

"No way," she said, exaggeratedly dragging out the two words.

"Yes. I can hardly believe it myself. Out of all the places for me to see him again. He cornered me out in the hall and expects me to go out with him tomorrow night."

She sat up straight in her chair. "It's fate. New York is huge. For you to see him again and so soon. It's meant to be. You so have to do it."

My immediate response was to shake my head no.

"Come on, Bails. Don't tell me you're into the cute,

dimpled Wilshire of the Park Avenue Wilshires? He was cute, but far too sweet."

I doubted with how things had gone that the guy would ever want to see me again. He hadn't even tried to kiss me goodnight or even suggest he'd call, which I'd been grateful for.

"Besides, Kalen's perfect. With the luck you're having, you'll run into that turd Scott and he'll see you with someone way hotter than he is."

The thought almost made me smile, but insecurities that ran too deep made me hesitate.

"Scott wouldn't care. He blames me for his cheating."

Outrage filled Lizzy's expression, but I cut her off before she could rant on my behalf. I decided to tell her a truth I'd kept to myself since the breakup.

"He said I was boring."

As my heart thudded in my chest at the embarrassing admission, she sat there open-mouthed.

"Boring how?" she asked.

I closed my eyes and found the ground, unable to look her in the eye when I said it.

"In bed."

I finally stopped picking at my nails and met her gaze.

"Okay, spill. What did he want you to do? A little bondage, maybe a spanking..."

I shook my head. Needing to free myself from what I'd been holding inside, I admitted, "He liked me to dress up in a short plaid skirt, a button-down shirt tied at the waist, and pigtails."

She chittered. "Really. I can totally see him asking for that. The guy was probably rejected by the head cheerleader in high school." She laughed at her joke. "But that's not all bad, if you're into that kind of thing."

I shrugged. "That wasn't a big deal. I was okay with that. It's when he asked me to call him Daddy that I drew the line."

My skin crawled at the thought. Saying that word made me think of my father and ewww, I just couldn't.

"Gross," she said. "I mean, to each his own. But just because you don't have daddy issues doesn't make you boring."

I nodded, though I didn't wholeheartedly believe it.

"Bails," she said, drawing my attention. "Scott and his tiny dick can't possibly compare to the *hotter than fuck* Kalen wanting to see you again."

"He wants to screw me again," I corrected.

"My point. He didn't think you were boring," she said.

"Maybe."

I got up. It was getting late and I needed to get to bed. I had work in the morning.

"You should see Kalen again."

I stared at my well-meaning best friend. "I'll think about it."

"Maybe fun with the hot Scot will break you out of your funk over the kinky Scott." I rolled my eyes at her play on words. "Even if you don't, the fact that Kalen wants you should cleanse you of no good Scott's excuse for being a straight-up asshole."

I wanted to believe her, but it was hard.

"Maybe..." I said.

I'd thought Scott was my future. Now he lived in our house with the woman he'd cheated on me with. I couldn't think about that if I wanted some sleep. I headed for my bedroom and tried my best not to dwell over the sex god who made my pulse race just by looking at him. Tomorrow was a new day. I needed to focus on my career and not sex, which had gotten me in trouble more times in my life than I liked to think.

My alarm blared, reminding me that I had a job. Getting out of bed wasn't easy. I felt almost drugged. I pushed through all the undecided feelings I had about seeing Kalen. Now was the time to make a name for myself in my chosen career and I couldn't afford to be late. It was my first day on a new assignment, and first impressions couldn't be taken back. I needed to impress the senior I'd be working under as well as the partner-in-charge.

In conservative slacks and top, I left after eating a bagel and drinking a steaming cup of tea. Lizzy hadn't been up. Then again, she owned her own art gallery and set her hours.

I barely made it on the train before the doors closed. Luck was on my side that morning, and I was happy to find that the car wasn't overly crowded.

My destination was already mapped as I'd done all the necessary background work on the client. Independence, which was mandated in order to perform an audit, meant I'd researched the CEO and board of directors to ensure that I didn't know anyone on a personal level.

The CEO was a stern-looking man who reminded me a lot of Lizzy's father, handsome but imposing. The board was composed of an older, hardened crew of people with long and impressive resumes.

Ready as I'd ever be, I arrived fifteen minutes before scheduled time at King Towers, one of the largest buildings in Manhattan in the heart of the financial district. It took five minutes to get through security and procure my new badge, but I was on the seventeenth floor, with ten minutes to spare.

Only, it appeared I was the last to arrive. So much for making an impression.

I pushed through the doors of the conference room we'd been assigned to and stumbled to a stop. The room lacked a view except for the wall of windows into the hallway. The oval table held a dozen chairs or so. But it was the man who stood that captured my attention.

"Bailey, I'm glad you could make it."

There before me, with sleeves rolled up as if he'd been at work for hours, stood my ex, Scott.

He proceeded to introduce me to the other team members, Anna, Jim, and Kevin. Though I'd plastered a smile on my face, I was in no way calm about having Scott there. It appeared he was the senior-in-charge.

I shouldn't have been surprised, considering his father was a partner in one of the largest firms in the world. I wanted to believe that I'd gotten my job on merit, but the truth was, being engaged to Scott probably helped. Scott had denied that when I'd asked, but it always bothered me.

"Bailey." I glanced up to see Scott way too close. When had he moved? "Can I talk to you a minute?"

Our colleagues pretended not to be interested in what we were saying, but they weren't doing a very good job.

I nodded and stepped out into the hall. It was a good thing the conference room was tucked away in a dark corner. There wasn't anyone milling around outside.

"Why are you here?" I hissed.

I'd hoped never to see him again.

He'd worked in the Boston office while I finished my degree. But once I graduated, we'd planned the move to New York. One of the firm's larger offices was here, which offered more opportunity for advancement. I thought it would be rare for our paths to cross with several hundred employees in New York alone. It appeared I was wrong.

"The senior assigned to this engagement was reassigned. I was brought in last minute," he said. That explained a lot. "I didn't see it as a problem since we are no longer together."

I swallowed. "It's not," I said, trying to appear unaffected.

"Good."

I turned to go back inside when his hand caught my arm. I waited for some kind of feeling to overcome me. But there was nothing like when Kalen touched me, which had burned through my skin like a brand.

"One more thing," Scott said.

I almost groaned but managed to hold it in. I glared at him instead until his hand fell away.

"Melissa wants the ring."

Talk about a jaw-dropping statement. Was he serious? It wasn't like I wanted the damn thing. I'd left in such a rush after I saw the text from her on his phone, I hadn't thought about the stupid ring. He'd been in the shower and I'd hurriedly packed a few things. My mind had been

48

on finding a hotel for the night and what I would do after.

I'd called out sick the next day and had gone back to move the precious little I'd accumulated while living out from under my father's rule. Until that moment, I hadn't realized I'd just moved under someone else's.

"You're a piece of work," I said by way of answer.

"Don't blame me. If you'd been even a decent lay, I wouldn't have had to go look for it elsewhere."

I clenched my fist and struggled not to punch him in his smug face. I spun on my heels and went into the room.

Scott, being the good liar he was, smoothly transitioned into senior-in-charge like he hadn't just insulted me.

I sat as far away from him as I could without it being too obvious as he went into speech mode.

"You are well aware of the rumors circling King Enterprises, specifically their private equity company."

I wouldn't have heard if not for Lizzy's parents bringing it up the other night. Growing up in what some would call the "simple life," technology wasn't ingrained in my life. Sometimes I forgot I had a cell phone.

"The board brought us in to independently audit the financials of that corporation and not the entire conglomerate. The board wants to prove to the SEC and King's clients that they have nothing to hide. Bringing us in as a firm without a stake in the larger audit pie makes our findings completely independent."

Scott then began to dole out our assignments, leaving me for last.

"Bailey, you'll be in charge of cash."

I ground my teeth together. Of course, he'd give me

grunt work. I would be responsible for getting confirmations from the bank to ensure that what was on their balance sheet matched what the bank reported. But it wasn't that simple. I also had to review the bank reconciliations for each of their cash accounts of which they had many. *Joy*, I thought and nodded without making a groan of protest.

I pulled out my laptop, having made a decision. I would see Kalen that night. Lizzy was right. I deserved to enjoy myself and not let a pond scum like Scott make me feel less of a woman. If he only knew that when I came that night, it would be my silent *fuck you* to the man I once thought I loved.

SEVEN

Though it had been a productive day, Scott didn't let us go on time. I was going to be late meeting Kalen.

The group asked if I wanted to join them for dinner. As Scott watched, I relished, saying for his benefit, "I'm sorry I can't tonight. I have a date."

His eyes had burned into mine as a disapproving line flattened his mouth. I didn't care and swept out of the room with a grin on my face until nervousness crept in. There was no time to go home and dress for the evening. Would Kalen still find me attractive free of makeup and dressed more like a librarian?

At the street, I hailed a cab. It wasn't an expense I took lightly if I planned to find a decent apartment and move out of Lizzy's place. But I didn't want to take a chance with the train.

Lucky for me, I quickly got a taxi. As I sat, I thought again about adding the Uber app to my phone as I gave the cabbie the name of the restaurant. He nodded without needing me to give him the address. The place was kind of famous and on the expensive side. Several TV shows and movies had been filmed there, so it wasn't unusual the cabbie knew the place by name.

The ride over proved unpredictable if you include a backup, an accident, and general traffic. I made it to Club 21 three minutes after eight. I paid the fair and was ushered in by the doorman. I stood at the hostess station at five minutes past the hour.

"I have a dinner reservation with—" I paused, realizing then that I didn't have Kalen's last name.

Being that this was the kind of place that required men to wear jackets, and jeans and sneakers weren't allowed, I felt foolish not to know Kalen's last name.

"Miss Bailey," the guy behind the podium said.

"Yes, how'd you know?"

Brought up a small-town girl, I was used to everyone knowing me. But this was New York.

"The gentleman said that when the most beautiful redhead walked in the door, her name would be Bailey and to bring her right up."

Flattered into speechlessness, I followed him up to the third floor and stopped dead in my tracks when we stepped into a private dining room with only one table, and one man who filled the room like no other.

Seeing him for the third time, still I was taken aback by just how beautiful he was. He stood near the table, and since I wasn't wearing four-inch heels, I got a real sense for just how tall he was.

Unable to hold his smoldering stare, I turned my head and got a sweeping view of the room. It was classically appointed with golden crown molding and expensive drapes that framed a fantastic view of Central Park. The lighting came from a large overhead crystal chandelier and wall sconces. The place could be a dining room in Lizzy's parents' house and felt just as intimate.

"You're wearing pants," he said, looking annoyed.

Startled, I turned to see that the host was gone and we were alone with the door closed. I looked down to see that I did, in fact, have pants on. I knew this, but he had a way of making me senseless and confused.

"Yes," I said, not sure what the problem was. If he only knew what a small victory it was to wear pants and loosen the hold a little more the community I'd grown up in had over me.

"Next time wear a skirt," he demanded, and I was jarred back to reality.

"Excuse me," I said, mustering all the incredulity I could in the face of such a gorgeous man. Surely, I'd misheard him. One, he said *next time* as if it were a foregone conclusion that there would be one. Two, he'd told me what to wear, like I was a possession he could control. It was too close to how I'd grown up. I fought against the urge to find the floor with my eyes and give in. "I'm not sure what your problem is, but I'll wear whatever I damn well want."

The curse slipped from my tongue, easier than I thought possible.

Undeterred, he stalked over to me, causing me to expel my breath. My body involuntarily shivered when his hand took mine.

"You could—wear what you wanted—or you could trust me and do as I ask."

I lifted my chin high, considering how much taller he was.

"Who said I would see you again after tonight?"

He brought my hand to his lips and a jolt of desire coursed from my arm, up to my shoulder, and down to my center to explode at my core.

He stepped back, giving me room to breathe. "Your choice, lass." He said the last with the knowledge that it turned me on. "You should know hiding yourself under this fabric means I can't touch you like I know you want me to."

My jaw dropped, not used to this type of forwardness. Yet, if I was honest with myself, he'd spoken the truth. I had come there to sleep with him, not anything more or less. His self-assuredness only added to my fantasy of how the night would go.

The waiter walked in with a bottle of wine before we could exchange any more words. Poor guy looked more flustered than me. Sexual tension was thick in the air and the waiter appeared unsure of whether he was about to get a tongue lashing for interrupting what surely looked like an intimate moment.

Kalen guided me to the table. Like a gentleman, he pulled out my chair and decorum dictated that I sit. Kalen took his seat across from me, never taking his eyes off me as the waiter approached.

True to his words from yesterday, he gave me his full and undivided attention. Though I didn't want to admit it, it made me feel special. Suddenly, the idea of wearing a skirt was very appealing as sexual liberation took hold inside of me.

"Your wine, sir," the waiter said, managing only to

sound slightly nervous. Kalen leaned back and allowed the guy to pour the wine into the waiting goblet. Kalen picked it up, eyeing it in the light before putting the glass to his beautiful lips.

Every movement he made sent a sexual thrill through me.

He nodded to the waiter before turning his attention back to me. The guy finished pouring Kalen's glass, and then moved to mine before leaving us alone again.

When I looked around for the menu, thinking the waiter had obviously made a mistake, Kalen said, "I took the liberty of ordering when you were late."

Feeling chastised, even though his tone had remained calm and pleasant the entire time, I said, "I was five minutes late. Well within the limits of polite society. Plus, it wasn't my fault. There was an accident and traffic."

He cut my blathering short and said, "In my business, five minutes is a lifetime."

Feeling off balance and more unnerved than ever in the presence of this man, I spoke as if I were a petulant child, "And what is it that you do?"

"Rule the world," he said, with a hint of amusement.

Before I could call him on his arrogance, a team of waiters arrived with our first course. The plate before me smelled heavenly and my stomach churned in anticipation, reminding me of my meager lunch.

He took his first bite, and his expression dared me to say something instead of eating. But when that bite touched his lips, I swore his expression was orgasmic and I had to taste the food to see if it was as good as it looked.

It was divine, and I ate, unable to decide if I'd ever had

something so good. It was like that commercial—finger-licking good. And I wanted to lick mine and then his. Instead, we finished our first course without any more conversation, but a whole lot of eye fucking, as Lizzy would say.

After the plates had been removed and the wait staff gone, he said, "So...tell me," he started, his blazing eyes boring into mine. I expected him to say something suggestive or even lewd the way his eyes left my face for a second to glance down to my cleavage before returning. "What do you do?"

Oh, I should have expected that. I mean, it was the obvious question, given I'd asked him first. But the way he pinned me with his gaze told a completely different story. In fact, I found myself tongue-tied, unable to speak the easy answer. My eyes drifted to his mouth and took in the most perfect, kissable lips I'd ever seen.

"Bailey," he said. And I watched his mouth form my name.

Blinking, I realized what I was doing. I was playing right into this man's hands. And oh, what magical hands he had. Our encounter had proven that. Moments too late to hide my attraction, I spoke. "I'm an accountant." I couldn't tell him I was an auditor. Most people automatically thought IRS. And hell, working for that agency was just as bad as being called a lawyer in some circles.

"Mmm." The noise he made shot directly to my center. All of a sudden, I felt heat course over my body in a rolling wave. I wanted to fan myself. But again, that would make it all too clear that he was getting to me.

"What about you? You weren't specific before," I asked

quickly, before I made a fool of myself. This man knew what effect he had on women—the smirk on his face said as much.

He picked up his wine glass, swirling the liquid around and hypnotizing me in the process. "I run a business," he said, sounding reluctant, as if he didn't want to tell me. He watched me like he was expecting some sort of reaction before placing the glass to his lips. And I found myself thinking about kissing him.

"What kind?" I probed, trying to steer this conversation far away from sex and my mind away from his inviting mouth. The way he continued to stare at me only made me more curious.

"A bit of this and a bit of that," he said, still watching me. I fidgeted in my seat. His eyes were like minefields, and I felt like I'd explode any minute.

Thankfully, the second course arrived, and all those thoughts were forgotten. The flavors of the food erupted in my mouth. I couldn't help myself—I moaned slightly and let my tongue dance over my lips to get at every last drop before I impatiently shoved more food into my mouth and embarrassed myself further. *Take it slow*. My parents had taught me better table manners.

When we finished the food in front of us, he spoke as if he'd plucked the thought from my brain. "If you lick your lips one more time, I will take you on this table instead of waiting until I get you to a bed."

He couldn't have timed his statement any better. Protest was again stifled by the appearance of the busboys, who removed our empty plates from the table. It was as if they had cameras watching us and were just waiting for our silverware to be put down. Looking up, I searched for tiny cameras until they left, after using what looked like a knife of some sort to gather any wayward crumbs off the white tablecloth.

When the well-choreographed team left, I spoke the first words that came to mind. "And what makes you think I'll be going home with you?"

He arched a brow, and his green eyes bore into mine. "I never said home."

I bit back a snarky retort. The ego this man had. *I wasn't good enough to take home?*

"Lass, your arousal is apparent on your pretty little face. You're flushed with desire and my dick is hard enough to cut diamonds. Dinnae pretend that you didn't come here so I could fuck you."

Waiters appeared with the next course as I'd been thunderstruck into silence, again.

With mixed emotions, I stabbed at the food placed in front of me, which I hadn't ordered. I wanted to dislike his choices, but the food was just as amazing, if not more, as the previous courses had been. I warred with wanting to moan at the taste and spit it out in objection. This man had ruled my every movement since I'd gotten there, and I'd let him.

I finished my food because it wasn't the chef's fault that I'd chosen to have dinner with an egomaniac. But Kalen was dead wrong if he thought he was getting me in bed that night. I wouldn't go anywhere with him, no matter how much my body fought against my brain.

He'd finish eating several bites before I had. When I swallowed my last, the tension in my body was coiled tight.

"Tell me, Bailey. Why are you dancing around why you came tonight? We both need to get this out of our system."

Outraged, I scooted back, seeking space away from him and his callous words. The table had rattled as if giving voice to my silence. I needed to get my wits about me, and I was out of my seat before he could ask where I was going.

"Leaving?" he asked with an imperious brow lifted.

Needing distance, I walked away but not to the door. Once again, he was right. I'd come to get fucked. I moved toward the opposite wall, wanting to regain my equilibrium.

I didn't make it very far before he was behind me. He was a mountain of a man who'd moved like a panther. I didn't know he was there until his warmth hit my back, along with his very apparent erection.

"Maybe I was wrong about your pants. They frame your ass in the most perfect way."

The heat of him melted me to my core, and I reached out a hand to the wall to steady myself. His hand wormed its way around my waist and long fingers unhooked my pants to give him more room to explore beneath the waistband. His fingertips brushed against forbidden places that sparked raging fires within me.

"This is what you came here for. For me to touch you, then fuck you."

I exhaled as he stroked over that bundle of nerves that sent me to orgasm heaven and beyond.

"I never said I would fuck you." The lie was born from defiance.

One long finger curled up and inside me.

"The crème that is coating my finger says something different," he said.

59

I wanted to say something, anything to deny what was true. But his skillful finger stroked in and out of me as his thumb rubbed circles over my clit. All I could do is pant, even as I heard the door open.

With just enough room to turn my head, I saw the team of waiters bring in our dessert course.

Kalen didn't seem to care. He didn't stop, and all I could do was bite my lip to muffle the moans that tried to escape. I whimpered and squirmed, embarrassed that they could tell what we were up to.

"Don't act shy. The way you're coating my finger, you're turned on more by the idea we're being watched. And if you'd worn a skirt, I could be inside you now with them none the wiser as to what is going on. Instead, you'll have to settle for this."

His fingers moved with more purpose as I crept closer and closer to the edge. When I detonated, I spasmed with a force I didn't think possible.

"That's it, lass," he whispered in my ear. "Even good girls can be bad. But our time will be short as I have somewhere to be. Fucking will have to wait for another night."

After I came down, I spun and hastily buttoned my pants, prepared to leave.

"You really should have dessert," he said, eyeing the plates that had been left on the table. "I think I'll have mine now."

The finger that had so expertly brought me to near tears in utter pleasure slipped between his lips like it was natural. He watched me as he sucked the taste of me from his finger.

It shouldn't have been erotic, but it was. I felt the flames of hell lick at my core as the devil himself stood before me like the sex god he was.

The smirk on his face convinced me to stalk over to the table and sit. I wouldn't let the chocolaty confection go to waste. Besides, the damn man had dared me to stay with those green eyes of his.

I jammed my fork into the gooey goodness, not sure what else to say or do.

He sat with the visible evidence of his arousal poking at the front of his slacks. I almost felt bad I'd gotten off and he hadn't. He lifted a hand and studied his watch as if he'd gotten a notification of some kind.

"I have to go," he said, lifting a finger in the air. Seconds later, the head waiter came bustling in, lending credence to there being cameras. Kalen's eyes twinkled as if he guessed what I was thinking. Heat rose in my cheeks, knowing we had been watched from beginning to end.

"Please wrap up dessert," he said to the guy, who took our plates without any preamble.

"So that's it," I said, feeling petulant.

"Time isn't something I have an abundance of. You were late, wearing pants and making fucking whatever this is out of us impossible. At least not tonight."

I opened my mouth to speak, but the waiter was back in record time with a bag that looked more like something they'd use at an expensive boutique and not a to-go bag.

"Charge the card on file," Kalen said.

The waiter nodded and disappeared. In that time, Kalen was up and helping me out of my chair.

"My driver will get you home," he said, ushering me out of the room.

If I thought he was riding with me, I was mistaken. He helped me into a luxury SUV, then handed me the bag with our uneaten dessert.

"Another time, Miss Glicks."

I sat dumbfounded as he closed the door and said something to the driver. How did he know my last name? Then I watched him get keys from a valet. But I didn't see the car he would get into as the driver asked, "Where am I taking you?"

He'd spoken in the same lyrical accent Kalen did, diverting my attention long enough for me to rattle off my address. By the time I looked back, Kalen was gone.

I was left to wonder what the hell had just happened.

EIGHT

"So," Lizzy said when I walked in the door. She was lounging on her favorite chair as usual. "How'd it go with Mr. Big Dick Shagger?"

I gaped. "How did you know he has a big dick?"

I didn't remember specifically mentioning that to her.

"Honey, the way you were walking yesterday, his stick had to be big."

Leave it to Lizzy to make me laugh when my life felt like it was spiraling out of control. She covered her mouth as we both giggled.

"Am I right or what?" she asked.

"Okay, fine. He's big, though I didn't actually see it."

I'd seen the outline through his pants and that was proof enough.

"Definitely fate. Are you going to screw him again?" she asked eagerly.

"Lizzy," I admonished.

"Don't be such a stick in the mud. If anyone deserves guilt-free sex, it's you."

I couldn't help but think about how I should have been a married woman living in the apartment Scott bought for us in a luxury high-rise on the Upper East Side.

"Tell me you're not thinking about that asshole."

I met her gaze. "How can I not?"

She lifted one finger. "First, he never deserved you. Second, he's like every other rich self-important asshole out there. They want a virginal wife but a whore as a mistress. That's why I don't date those assholes."

Scott hadn't exactly been rich like Lizzy's family. But he'd never wanted for anything.

"Maybe if I'd been better in bed—"

She cut me off. "Don't you go there. It's not your fault."

"But maybe—"

She shook her head. "No, Bails. He's at fault."

"Remember, he said I was boring."

I couldn't quite get over that.

"Boring," she repeated murderously. "He blamed you for him cheating because you were boring in bed. That was something he would have figured out a couple of years ago. He's just using that as an excuse."

"Maybe." Unfortunately, I lacked the confidence she had.

———

I WOKE UP FEELING LIKE I WAS STILL CAUGHT IN MY dream. My back felt very warm, and there was a hard mass pressed against the crevice of my ass. When I shifted a little, prepared to get up to see what was behind me, a hand gripped my thigh and a warm breath of air caressed my neck.

What the hell? Had I let Kalen come home with me last night? No, I hadn't. Freaked out, I shot out of bed, stumbling to my feet. Looking back, I recognized that wavy blond hair and penetrating blue eyes.

"Matt, what the hell are you doing?" I said exasperatedly.

With dimples showing, he smiled at me lazily. "Come back to bed, peanut."

Jaw dropped, I stared at him. "Why are you in my bed?"

Technically, it wasn't my bed.

"This is my room," he said with a smirk.

Though he lived in Chicago, he and his sister owned the apartment together.

"You don't live here," I spouted back and crossed my arms over my chest.

He stretched and yawned as he said, "My name on the deed says otherwise."

My eyes nearly crossed as I rolled them and huffed out a breath. I threw my hands in the air and made my way around the bed to the other side of the room, toward the bathroom. I was sidelined when he tugged my arm and tumbled me back into bed with his strong arms around my waist.

From where I lay on my back I stared up at him as he said, "Don't be mad, peanut. It's cold. And you're warm. I'm only here a couple of days, and then you'll have the room back to yourself."

Matt was a fun-loving guy. The kind a girl could crush on and I had. Lizzy's twin was hot. But his playful flirts had come days too late. When I'd thought it was Kalen spooning me, my inner sex demon had grinned, only to be disappointed when I realized who it was.

Snarkily and filled with humor, I said, "I am not sharing a room with you. I'll sleep on the couch."

I couldn't very well ask him to sleep there. It was his place.

He pouted and said, "No way. I'd much rather share a bed with you. I promise not to take advantage." He winked. "Besides, I hear you're finally rid of that asshole. So what's the problem?"

The problem was, I might have relished his attention two days before. Now, I couldn't stop thinking of the egomaniac. And as much as I'd like to forget my former life, I wasn't a girl who slept around.

"I can't share a bed with you. Waking up with your..." I gestured toward his nether regions, "pressed against me wouldn't be fair to either one of us."

"Oh, my boner you mean," he said, laughing.

I turned my head away, but his hand came to my chin and gently turned me to face him. "That's a guy thing. But even if it weren't morning, I'd still have a hard-on being next to you. It's just a fact. It does that when I'm next to a beautiful woman."

There was no way I could do this. I slapped his hands off my thighs and scrambled away again. "You're such a flirt," I stated.

He just flashed me his pearly whites before yawning again. As he stretched some more, his muscles flexed and bunched, and I couldn't help admiring him.

Lizzy's brother had it all—looks, money, and charm. I'd

crushed on him my freshman year of college in Boston, before I met Scott. And after sophomore year, Matt transferred to the University of Chicago.

"If you don't mind, I have to get ready for work," I said.

Turning, I hurried inside the attached bathroom. Just as I was about to close the door, he said, "Peanut?"

Peeking out the door again, I stared at him.

"Nice shirt."

Looking down, I realized I'd gone to sleep in my normal pajamas, a plain tee shirt that barely skimmed the bottom of my ass. I hadn't expected company, though.

Rolling my eyes, I closed the door, trying to collect myself.

It wasn't until after my shower that I realized I didn't have a robe or a change of clothes. Opening the door a crack, I saw Matt's back and the slow rhythm of his breathing. Tiptoeing out, I walked into my closet and closed the door, dismayed that there wasn't a lock. After I got dressed, I grabbed my messenger bag, which held my firm-issued laptop and other things needed for the job.

Lizzy's door was closed, and I had to leave soon to make it to work on time. Unwilling to be late, I passed her door, vowing that she and I would have a talk when I got home. Had she known her brother was coming and didn't tell me? It wasn't like I'd planned to stay here forever. But maybe I should stay at a hotel while Matt was here? He was a complication I didn't need. It was bad enough I was headed to work with my ex. And why hadn't I told Lizzy that yet?

Fear. Maybe. Then again, I had a certain someone on the brain.

Lucky for me, Scott wasn't there when I arrived. We got

a message that he was checking in on another project and would be in later that afternoon. Meanwhile, I wondered if I'd ever get a look at the elusive King brothers.

"Do you ever wonder if one of the guys you pass in the hall is a King?" Anna, my co-auditor, asked.

Since she'd caught me watching the limited foot traffic down our hall, I had to laugh.

"Honestly, yes. I mean, isn't it weird no one knows what they look like?"

"I know, right?" she said.

Work was grueling, and by the end of the day, I was ready to go home. I stepped into the bathroom on my way out.

"Oh, hey there," Anna said when she came into the bathroom. "Scott is looking for you."

"Really?" I questioned, confused as to why he would be. I cleaned up my supplies and put them back into my purse.

"Yeah, we're all headed out to grab a bite to eat at Sully's," she said.

I wasn't in the mood. I wanted an early night and lots of sleep. "I really should get home."

In addition, the last thing I wanted to do was spend any more time with Scott than I had to. My co-workers had no idea of my history with the man, or so I thought, leaving me unwilling to bring up that excuse.

She shrugged and said, "We don't bite. But it's cool," before heading into a stall.

Finished washing my hands, I headed out. Did the team think that I was avoiding them or too good to hang out? *Not good.* I was new and hadn't yet made any friends. Not that I needed to. But I at least wanted to get along with them. It wouldn't be good for me to alienate them. I closed my eyes a second, thinking it wouldn't hurt for me to go for a few minutes.

"There you are," Scott said just as I was about to bump into him. I opened my eyes to find him studying my face with concern. "Tired?"

It wasn't a question. Three years of togetherness and he knew me pretty well, and I hated that he sounded like the guy I'd fallen in love with.

"Yes," I said, nodding. I moved to sidestep him, but he blocked me.

"The ring," he said, all business.

I scoffed, rolling my eyes at my idiocy. Of course, he hadn't cared about me. He'd used that as a prelude to what he really wanted.

"I'll look for it," I said, annoyed.

It wasn't like I wanted it. But I also didn't want the woman he cheated on me with to have it either.

"What the hell does that mean?" he asked.

Beyond the barrier of the glass-enclosed conference room, the two remaining team members glanced up and Scott checked himself. He straightened, adding some distance between us, and lowered his voice.

"Why don't you know where it is?" he asked.

I glared at him like I could kill him with my stare. "I don't know, Scott," I said in a stage whisper, knowing we had eyes on us. "Somehow, finding out my fiancé cheated on me didn't inspire me to care about the stupid thing. I think I tossed it when I packed my things. Maybe it's in Boston."

I left him standing there, jowls flapping in the wind.

Upon entering, Jim smiled. "We're all headed to Sully's if you want to join us." His eyes strayed behind me where I had been a second before. I'd hoped Scott had left. But when the door opened again, he came in followed by Anna.

The awkwardness that filled the room could be cut with a knife.

"Sure. I can't stay long," I added.

That seemed to smooth out the air as everyone smiled except for Scott. A win for me.

"I'm going to head home," he said.

I resisted blowing out a sigh of relief. Still, exhausted from a long day and little sleep the night before, I vowed I'd have the one drink.

The problem was, I'd found an anomaly in one of the bank accounts. If Scott hadn't been such a jerk, I would have brought it to his attention. Tomorrow. He was my boss on this project whether I liked it or not. One hour tops at Sully's and then home. I'd find that stupid ring and decide just what to do. I wondered if I shoved it up his rear if his girlfriend would still want it.

NINE

SULLY'S WAS FAIRLY CROWDED WITH HAPPY HOUR IN full swing. Everyone in attendance was clad in suits and other business attire, outside of the bartenders and wait staff.

With dark wood and old-fashioned touches, the place felt homey in the dim light as we walked into a large bar area. It spanned the entire width of the back wall. Booths lined the other two walls, and a few sat before the front windows. High bar tables filled in the middle.

We claimed a booth on the far left side, and I found myself taking a step up to take a seat planted on a platform. I hoped to sit next to Anna, but she was herded by Jim to sit next to him and opposite me. That left Kevin to scoot in beside me.

We spent a little time looking at the menu when Anna cleared her throat.

"So, I'm just going to ask," she began. "What's going on with you and Scott?"

There it was. Scott hadn't exactly been subtle when he

pulled me to the side to interrogate me. Also, it wasn't a secret. We had plans to marry. Invitations had been sent out, including to some of our co-workers. Yes, most were in Boston, but news traveled fast.

"We were engaged. Now we're not."

I shrugged, hoping to end all conversation.

Anna squinted. "Is that allowed?"

I couldn't blame her for her curiosity.

"Not if we were still engaged. But we're not. Besides, he wasn't originally assigned to this project and things happen. We're adults and we'll get through it."

I flagged the waiter, hoping to derail any further questioning. Thankfully, Anna got the message as the waiter arrived. My phone buzzed and there was a text from Lizzy.

Come home now, it read.

I glanced up and noticed everyone looking at me, including the waiter.

"I'm sorry, guys. Something's come up. I have to go."

I scooted out of the bench after Kevin moved out. I said a hasty goodbye and went to hail a taxi. I really needed to get that Uber app. Luckily, yellow cabs were in abundance. I wondered if Uber was the cause.

I rushed in the door, expecting to find the house on fire or Lizzy half dead. Instead, she sat at the kitchen island absently studying an overflowing vase of orange roses.

"What's up?" I asked, unsure what was going on.

Had something happened to her parents, her brother?

It took her a second before she met my eyes. She held out a small white card that was in her hand.

I took it and read.

Tonight 7:30pm Eventi Hotel

"I just got home," Lizzy said. "I'm pretty sure that's not for me."

Once I saw it was signed with the initial K, I agreed.

I glanced at my phone. It was twenty minutes passed seven.

"I'll never make it," I said, though I wasn't sure who I was talking to, Lizzy or myself.

"Sure you can," she said.

She hurried to her feet and dragged me to her bedroom. Though I could wear some of Lizzy's clothing, the fact was she was tall and statuesque, and I was the opposite. I couldn't fit in everything she owned.

She started tossing out clothes as she scoured her closet for something she felt I should wear. I picked up the remains and refolded and rehung, unable to tamp down my neat freak side.

"This," she said, holding out a sleek and streamlined, black formfitting V-neck midi dress with a swath of ribbed fabric at the waist for a bit of detail. "Hurry."

Because it was made from stretchy material, it would probably work. I rushed to my room and tossed off my clothes, leaving them in a pile much like the one Lizzy made in her room. Then I pulled the dress over my head, ignoring the designer label. It probably cost more than some people's rent, and I couldn't think about that or I'd be late.

Based on my conversations with Kalen the previous night, he didn't accept any excuse for tardiness.

I stopped. What was I doing? I would be late. My luck he wouldn't be there.

"What are you doing?"

I glanced up to see Lizzy. "What's the point? I'm never going to make it in time."

She tsked me. "You'll make an entrance." She handed over a pair of heels. Funny. We were close in shoe size. The red sole platform patent leather heels were the perfect touch. I slid them on.

"I ordered you an Uber," she explained, handing me a tote bag.

"What is this for?"

"To drop in your purse and makeup bag. I also tossed in a pair of flats for when you come home in the morning."

She gave me a little wink.

This was crazy. But I found myself in the Uber reapplying makeup. Though I longed for my bed, sharing one with Kalen had an unexpected thrill running through my belly.

TEN

KALEN WAS LEAVING THE HOTEL WHEN I ARRIVED. I cinched the tie of the wool coat I snagged on my way out the door and went to intercept him.

Impeccably dressed in an overcoat that opened enough to reveal a tailored suit, he stopped when he noticed me.

As he approached, he said, "Late again, I see. Habit?"

My spine stiffened. The conceit of this man.

"For the record, I'm normally a punctual person when given adequate notice."

"I believe I sent the invitation hours ago."

I glared at him as he continued to get closer.

"I'm sorry. I guess I should have been waiting with bated breath for your flowers to arrive. But some of us have to work."

His brow lifted as my sarcasm dripped with disdain as he stopped before me. The frost in the air seemed to melt at his nearness.

"It's cold out, Miss Glicks. Allow me to give you a ride home."

His panty-melting accent momentarily distracted me again from the knowledge that he knew my last name.

"So that's it? I'm fifteen minutes late and date canceled."

With his eyes hidden in shadow, so dark on mine, they were unreadable.

"Need I remind you that fifteen minutes is everything, Miss Glicks. I'll need every second we have together to fuck you out of my system."

Jaw slackened, I stood there as he walked by me. When I turned, he was standing with a door open on a sleek midnight blue car.

"It's cold, Miss Glicks."

"What the hell is up with the Miss Glicks?" I said, heaving frigid air in and out. The man knew how to push my buttons and make me curse, which was quickly becoming a habit.

"Okay, lass," he said, the corner of his mouth twitched and left it slightly lifted in what might have been a grin.

"I don't need a ride," I said stubbornly. "I'll find my own way home. I'm a big girl."

He shrugged. "I dinnae ken one way or the other."

"De nay kin?" I asked. My confusion made my pronunciation drag and it was so far off.

"Get in the car," he said in a way that didn't brook an argument.

Damn him for his nonchalance when I couldn't get him out of my head either. I didn't have to speak whatever language he was to figure out what he meant.

When he started to close the door, I stomped in his direction. Why should I pay for a taxi? It was his invitation that brought me out tonight. *Oh, the lies we tell ourselves.*

I slipped into the seat and sank in the supple leather. The door closed and he rounded the car. I couldn't help but admire the beauty of the man who sat in the driver's seat.

"How did you know my last name?" I asked as he shifted into traffic.

"Your doorman greeted you and my driver overheard."

"And he reported it to you."

It wasn't a question. I'd hardly spoken to the man as I recalled the interaction.

"Is there a secret to knowing your last name?"

I whipped my head in his direction. "I guess it seems unfair when I don't know yours."

Slowly, he turned his head to eye me from head to toe, knocking me off balance. My coat might have been tied at the waist, but it gaped open enough at the top and between my legs to show skin that was exposed by the design of the dress.

His eyes met mine and he said, "It's Brinner."

Kalen Brinner. What an unusual name for a gorgeous but unusual man.

Then he turned, pulling into traffic, only to be immediately stopped at a red light. Way too soon it turned green, giving me only a view of his beautiful yet unreadable profile.

He left me off balance. Though he'd suggested he was only interested in me for sex, his casual perusal of my body hadn't registered approval or disdain, leaving me feeling embarrassed.

I straightened in my seat to close my coat. Goosebumps

had erupted over my skin from his stone-cold gaze. But just as I reached the gap at my legs, his hand stopped me. His fiery palm landed on my thigh and headed for the juncture between my legs.

My gasp was nothing compared to the moan that escaped me when his fingers brushed over my wet center. I'd chosen to go bare to avoid a panty line.

He too was surprised as his expression finally showed a reaction before his eyes found the road again. But that quick glance had revealed a hungry gaze.

"Show me," he commanded.

I was momentarily shocked by his request.

"Use my fingers to touch yourself," he said while rubbing tiny circles around my clit but avoiding making nail-biting contact.

The man was certainly skilled and didn't need my guidance to make me come as he'd proven the other night. Yet a second later, he demonstrated just that with a flick of his finger. It connected with my clit in a way that caused me to suck in a lungful of air. Then his touch was gone.

"If you want to get off, you'll have to use my fingers or wait until you get into your bed alone and fantasize about me."

Pissed, I tried to move his hand away, but it clamped down over my mound like a chastity belt. Unfortunately, his grip didn't brush the most sensitive parts.

Spying the bulge in his pants, I suddenly felt powerful. If I used him to get me off on the ride home, he'd be the one left to fantasize about me.

When had I gotten so bold? Scott had made me feel

useless and unwanted. Kalen, on the other hand, made me feel sexy and daring.

Feeling brave, I undid the sash and parted my coat to give me room. Then I snaked a hand over my parting thighs to cover his. I gripped two of his fingers to rub through my wetness and over my nub. I had to bite my tongue to keep my wanting sounds to a minimum. It didn't take much. His large hand was the perfect size, and with my perfect pressure, I was brought to the precipice in record time.

I was so close; I could come at any moment. He must have sensed that, taking over and stroking once over my clit, down my slit to plunge into my soft depths.

"Oh," I said, in little more than a breathy whisper.

He stroked in and out of me with an expertise he could patent.

"Take your coat off, climb into my lap, and let me finish you off."

Shyness crept in as I noticed the cars around us. I'd been all in a second ago without regard to who might see. But now, his request, which was crazy by the way, made me notice the traffic going past us. The late hour meant we weren't at a standstill, but there was still a fair amount of vehicles on the road. If anyone looked over...

"Or you could wrap those red lips of yours around my dick, lift that pretty ass of yours up in the air, and we could both get off."

Damn his suggestions. I wanted nothing more than his big cock inside of me. Was it foolish? Could he drive while I rode him?

"What about a condom?" I blurted.

He didn't bother to look at me, still navigating the car.

"We are nearly out of time, Miss Glicks. You will have to believe me when I tell you I'm clean and have the test results to prove it. Just as I will have to trust you are too. It's now or never."

His straightforwardness made me trust him, or it was just reckless need that won over rational thought. I stripped out of my coat, unbuckled my seat belt, and turned to find his cock straining against his pants. I went to work to free it and even went as far as to lick my tongue over the swollen tip as it sprang free. He too wore no underwear.

His hand gently pressed on the back of my head so I would take him deeper into my mouth. I obliged, though quickly insecurity filled me. He was so big, my teeth grazed over him and I wasn't sure he'd like it. I sat up and at his nod crawled over to straddle him.

I had an urge to kiss him, but decided it was more important for his eyes to be on the road. I inched down as he guided his head against my opening until I was fully seated on him.

He cursed in a language I didn't understand. But something about the way he said it made its meaning universal.

"Fuck yourself," he said way too calmly.

I would so analyze that a million different ways later. But at that moment, I was so filled with desire, I rocked myself up and down his shaft. His girth stretched me to the max as I rolled my hips some, wanting contact against my clit. Once I found the right angle, my internal magic button was activated, and I jacked myself off on him until I came apart around him.

Thank God I'd tamed my hair that morning. Otherwise,

he might not have seen around my wayward curls when I buried my head in the crook of his neck.

He, however, wasn't done. A master of multitasking, he gripped my waist so he could move me up and down at his pace as I sagged against him. I was still panting over my first orgasm as another one built. He powered into me like it was mission-critical that he come hard too.

His final grunt rocketed another orgasm out of me. I couldn't move when it was over as he held me tightly to him. I wanted to read more into the gesture, but my guess was that position made it easier for him to drive.

I'd almost fallen asleep, his cock still deep inside me when he said, "We're here, lass."

I felt the car move to the side and stop. Who had seen us? Had we been caught on film? That shouldn't have been my first question. Had he done that before? How the hell had he driven the car with me bouncing on his dick? But he'd managed the impossible.

Then the next question hit me. Was this it? Had he fucked me out of his system? Because as foolish as it was, he'd fucked me into his. No, I didn't love him. But I wasn't ready for the madness to end.

"You should go inside," he said quietly.

Oh, how dumb had I been to think he might have said something more romantic. A safer bet was he was done with me.

With as much dignity as I could muster, I raised myself off him. The emptiness I felt was more than the loss of his dick. By the time I made it in my seat, he had his monster cock hidden back in his pants.

"Yeah...um...thanks for the ride."

I couldn't even laugh at my accidental double entendre. I turned my back to him and opened the door as he idled at the curb. Outside, I pulled my dress down so I wouldn't flash any pedestrians.

Before I could close the car on my shame, he finally spoke.

"Miss Glick." As much as I didn't want to, I faced him, keeping my features schooled as impassively as I could. I waited a beat and then he added, "Sleep tight."

I closed the door on his smirk. *Miss Glicks.* Not lass or Bailey. Why the hell did I want to cry? Because I was a fool. Kalen Brinner was a player and I'd been played. *Well done, Bailey. You've certainly earned your scarlet S now.*

ELEVEN

Lizzy was nowhere to be seen when I walked in, until the door closed.

She popped her head out of her room and said, "You're home," stating the obvious. "Give me a second."

I took off my coat and hung it in the closet. By the time I took a seat in the living room, she was there.

"Don't leave me in suspense... Wait. You weren't gone very long."

I sighed. "No, it seems Kalen is a stickler on time."

"Oh," she said, pouting. "He wasn't there."

My hair tumbled over my shoulder and to my back as I shook my head no.

"He was there, all right. Grumpy as ever."

"Grumpy but gorgeous?"

I laughed because that was so true.

"Yes, grumpy but gorgeous. He started off giving me a lecture about being late." As her jaw opened, I finished with, "But I shut that one down. He ended up driving me home as I fucked him."

Her eyes narrowed as her head angled some. "Is that a metaphor?"

I blew strands of hair out of my face. "No. He drove as I straddled his lap and fucked him."

Her mouth opened before laughter filled the air.

"Way to go, champ. My little Bails has gone full slut mode. I'm so proud of you."

I groaned and covered my face with my hands. "What have I done?"

Her giggles didn't subside. "Don't shame yourself, girl. Be proud. You've taken control of your sexuality and had fun. But I really would like to hear more about moving car sex. It sounds intriguing."

Needing to free myself of the burden, I told her. "I wouldn't have believed it myself, but it happened."

She tapped a finger against her lips. "You know, I think I've heard of someone else doing it. It was on a highway in the middle of the night with little traffic, but go you. I'm actually a little jealous."

"Don't be," I said, sagging on the sofa. "He didn't ask me for my phone number. Only told me to sleep tight. And what does that mean? How do you sleep *tight*?"

"It's a saying," she said.

"I know," I whined. I wasn't that backwards with my church upbringing. "But what does it even mean?"

She shrugged and I let my head fall to rest on the back of the sofa. The phone rang and she walked over to answer the wall-mounted contraption that allowed the doorman to communicate with the residence.

She listened before saying, "Send him up."

It was my turn to let my mouth hang open. Was he here?

"Don't worry. It's a delivery guy," she said, reading me perfectly.

I checked the time. "Who would be delivering at this hour? Did you order something?"

She pursed her lips. "No."

We eyed the door suspiciously as if a mass murderer would knock at the door any second. When it came, we both jumped and eyed each other before Lizzy took bold steps toward the door. It was stupid to let fear grab hold of us. Who could possibly want to target us? Yet...

Behind the door, a teen with brightly colored hair and makeup to match held up a bag.

"Bailey Glicks," she said to Lizzy.

Curious, I stood, wondering what this delivery was about. The delicious smell, however, was telling. Yet I hadn't ordered any food.

"I'm Bailey."

The girl smirked at me before stepping forward, but Lizzy didn't budge. Teen or not, this was New York and Lizzy didn't let her through the door.

I held out my hand, wondering what she knew that I didn't. When I reached her, she dumped the bag in my hand.

"Enjoy," she said, spinning on her combat boots and leaving without waiting for a tip.

"What was that about?" Lizzy asked, watching the girl make her way to the elevator before softly closing the door.

"I don't know," I said, setting the bag on the island and slowly opening it.

On top lay an envelope. I snagged it and hopped up on a stool. Lizzy came over to lean over my shoulder.

"What does it say?" she asked.

I read it out loud. "My plans for tonight were to feed you before fucking you. I always make good on my promises. –K."

That explained the smirk on the teenage delivery girl's face. The envelope hadn't been sealed and she'd obviously peeked at the note.

The question was if the handwritten note had been penned by his hand. When did he have the time?

"Well, well, well," Lizzy began. "The man scores points for being a gentleman."

I arched an eyebrow. "I thought you didn't like nice guys."

Not that I thought Kalen was nice. He was demanding and sexy all wrapped into one. A word like "nice" didn't come into play.

"For me, no," she said emphatically. "For you, yes. You deserve a guy who thinks about your needs and not his own like that jackass Scott."

I thought back to my dinner with Kalen the night before when he'd gotten me off without asking for me to take care of him.

"He didn't leave his number," I said.

Lizzy pointed to the bottom of the note. There was an email address printed above my home address.

"I bet that's his. He must have ordered online."

"Yeah, and what am I supposed to do with that?"

My tech skills were limited.

She snagged the paper from my hand. "Does he have an iPhone?"

I shrugged, not knowing the answer. I didn't remember ever seeing his phone.

"Where's your phone?" she asked.

I did have one, though it was two generations old. Scott had bought it for me a couple of Christmases ago.

"What are you going to do with it?" I asked.

Remembering that Scott bought the device made me want to hurl it across the room until I remembered my bank account balance. I'd have to check my budget and see if I could afford a new phone. It wasn't like I cared if I had the latest and greatest. But I would upgrade if it meant I didn't have to keep something the jerk had given me.

"You could text him," she said, breaking into my thoughts.

"How?"

I only used mine for the basic features. Which was probably the reason Scott hadn't gotten me a new one.

"If he has an iPhone, you can use an email address like a phone number," she said.

"Why would I want to do that?"

My stomach growled, reminding me I hadn't eaten dinner.

"So," she began exaggeratedly, "You can take control of this relationship."

"It's not a relationship."

Her eye roll hit the ceiling before landing on me again.

"Not the point. He's dictated everything so far. Texting him will give you an advantage."

"Why?"

After two failed ones, it was clear I had no idea how relationships worked.

"Because he won't expect it," she said.

I pulled out my phone and stared at it. Did I really want to do this? Maybe I should leave well enough alone.

"Not yet," she said. "Eat first. Then you can tell him thank you for the delicious meal."

I didn't question her. I was starving anyway. Plus, what would the unflappable Kalen do if I texted him?

The meal, in fact, was delectable. It was like the man could read my mind and knew what I would like. And maybe he could. He already knew how to get me off like no man before.

Even though there had been more than enough to share, Lizzy had turned down the food. She'd gotten a text from Hans and had gone to her room. Knowing her, they were on a video call ogling each other.

After eating, I took the plunge and sent Kalen a text. If it didn't go through, Lizzy had suggested sending an email. But my **thanks for dinner** message appeared to have been sent. I set the phone down when I went to take a shower, trying not to worry if he would text back.

TWELVE

I LET OUT A SHRIEK WHEN I WALKED INTO THE bedroom with only a towel around me.

Matt stood there with a sexy grin on his face.

Footsteps thundered in my direction, and before I could ask him what he was doing, Lizzy appeared in the doorway with a gun in her hands.

I almost raised both of mine, but remembered that I was gripping the towel. I held up the other.

"What the hell is going on?" Lizzy cried, lowering the gun.

I let out a long, deep breath as my heart raced from the shock of seeing Matt and then seeing Lizzy with a gun.

"I was going to grab a shower," Matt said, feigning innocence.

"I was in the shower," I said, glowering at him.

His smile only grew wider. "I know, darling. That's why I'm standing here and not there," he said, pointing to the bathroom.

"Matt, give it up. Bails isn't interested."

"How do you know?" he said, winking at me.

I bit my lip, because he was so stinking cute. And if I were any other girl, I might have taken him up on his offer. But I wasn't.

Matt was a player with a capital P. For as long as I'd known him, he hadn't had a girlfriend. He didn't, however, lack for company in his bed. He could have been my one mistake, but that honor I'd given Kalen. I wouldn't repeat that experience again.

Ignoring Matt's seductive gaze, I turned my attention to Lizzy.

"What's with the gun?"

I wasn't afraid of them. My father had a few. But we lived in the country where occasionally wild animals if hungry enough would sneak into our camp for scraps.

"Matt got it for me," she said sheepishly.

"And I gave you lessons on how to use it. It's New York," he said.

Matt was a cop. It made sense.

"I'm going to grab a shower," he added.

"You can use mine," Lizzy offered.

She must have caught my indecision.

"My stuff is in there. Don't worry. I'll sleep on the couch," he said. "Unless you've changed your mind."

I glanced heavenward as I shook my head.

He laughed as he closed the door to the bathroom.

I opened my mouth to speak, thinking about the clothes I'd left on the floor, but didn't. My bra and panties wouldn't be the first he'd seen.

"I'm sorry about that," Lizzy said, gun pointing at the floor.

"What's there to be sorry for? It is his room. I'll sleep on the couch."

"Don't. You can share my room."

I shook my head. "It's fine. Your couch isn't the worst thing I've slept on."

I'd grown up sleeping on beds made of straw. Everything we had was made by hand or gotten from trade. Mattresses weren't a necessity.

"He's leaving tomorrow," she said.

"It's fine. Really. I should be looking for my own place."

"Bails," Lizzy said, fear on her face. "You don't have to go. In fact, I really like you here."

"Thanks. But I've intruded long enough."

I'd never lived alone. From sharing one small room with my sisters, to sharing a dorm room, to living with Scott, I'd never been alone. As scary as the thought was, it was also a little exciting.

"I should get dressed before your brother gets out."

She nodded and reluctantly left. I scrambled to the drawers to find something to put on. I'd barely pulled on one of my old cotton nightgowns I hadn't worn in years when the bathroom door opened.

Matt stopped in his tracks and eyed me.

"My God. You look like a Puritan."

I tried to laugh it off. Modesty was required in our community. The nightgown covered from my neck to my toes. Scott hadn't approved, but I couldn't throw them all away. They were a reminder of home. Something I could put on in the safety of my room when I got homesick.

"It's warm," I said, unable to explain to Matt why such barriers were needed.

Water sluiced down his chest to the towel wrapped around his waist. He was a fine specimen of a man, but that pull I felt toward Kalen and sin, wasn't there between Matt and me.

"You know, it's actually kind of hot. It makes me wonder what's under it."

My breath hitched. That wasn't what was supposed to happen.

He stepped closer, too close.

"Bailey," he said my name full of promise.

"Matt, we can't."

I wanted to step back, but his warm hands cupped my cheeks as his forehead dipped to meet mine.

"Why not? I've wanted you for a long time and I've seen how you've looked at me."

"So what, we have this one night and you leave and go back to Chicago and our friendship is ruined."

"Bailey," he said. "I came to New York because of you."

"What?" I repeated with a hitch in my throat. I'd crushed on him forever, but he'd never paid me any attention, other than being his sister's best friend.

"I think I've always liked you. Probably since the first day I saw you in my sister's room."

"But you ignored me," I retorted, trying to make sense of what he was saying, even though it was clear.

"Yeah, I was a bastard. I knew I wasn't ready to settle down. I never wanted to hurt you, and if I'd asked you out back then, I would have. So I waited."

"You waited too long," I said, realizing more than ever there was someone else I was interested in.

"Yeah," he huffed. "That bastard sank his hooks in you,

and I tried to warn you, but you didn't listen." He paused. "Sorry, I'm not trying to throw that in your face."

He was right, but so wrong. Scott was the past.

"But you left," I said, because he'd transferred to the University of Chicago after his sophomore year.

"Yep, and you two were pretty serious. I thought I'd lost my chance. And hadn't I? You were going to marry him, according to what Lizzy told me this summer. Then I got a call from her saying that you'd left him."

"But you didn't come for Christmas," I said, thrown completely off by this conversation.

He sighed. "You know things aren't right with my dad and me. He still doesn't like the idea that I don't want to take over the family business. That I want to be a cop."

"You should have come home," I said. *And not for me*, I thought. I knew firsthand that his parents were crushed by his retreat from the family.

"I know, but I'm here now. For you, I'd be willing to try a relationship. I haven't had one of those in a long time, but you're worth it."

This was all too much.

I stepped back. "It could never work. When would we see each other?"

"You could come to Chicago."

I gaped at him. "We barely know each other."

"I've known you for years," he said, his hands finally dropping to his sides.

"Not this way."

There had been that one kiss. I closed my eyes, trying to forget. Then I moved to the door.

"No," he said, giving up way too easily. "You take the

93

bed. I have a feeling I'm not going to sleep for a while anyway."

It suddenly felt weird between us.

I shook my head. "It's your room."

"No. It's yours," he said, sounding a little sad.

He bent and grabbed his duffle before leaving the room. And dumbly I wondered if I'd made the biggest mistake of my life. I knew Matt, and there was an attraction between us. Yet, I didn't want to move to Chicago. Kalen was a total mystery and had made no move to see me again. Why couldn't I be the girl who just looked for fun and not a happily ever after?

I flopped on the bed and pushed all thoughts of Kalen out of my mind. As I began to drift off to sleep, I remembered my phone. Had he texted me back?

THIRTEEN

Sleep had been fleeting. I gave up on it around dawn and got ready for work. I slipped out of the apartment and took the subway across town.

As I sat, I pulled up the one sentence reply Kalen had texted. It had played over in my head the entire way to work. I wasn't sure what I'd wanted him to say. But what I got was exactly what I'd expected.

In order to stop thinking about it, I immersed myself deep in work. Since I was the first to arrive, there were no distractions to keep me from my goal. Something was wrong with the bank accounts and I was determined to find it.

I didn't notice when Scott arrived until he leaned down and whispered in my ear, making me jump.

"You wanted to talk?" he asked.

I did. "Outside."

For some unknown reason, I didn't want to discuss it in front of the group.

I followed him out.

He folded his arms over his chest and stood there like the self-righteous prick he was.

Inwardly, I breathed. "I think I might have found something."

He dropped his hands, surprised at what I just said. "What?"

I explained how there were mysterious transfers of money in the tens of thousands of dollars, which in the scheme of things was nothing. They had been recorded as transfers to investment accounts. So far, I hadn't found the account where the money was going.

"This is a big company with many different corporations within the conglomerate. Maybe the money was transferred to one of the other corporate investment accounts," he explained.

"Maybe. I'll ask the accountant to show verification that it went into other company bank accounts."

"The amount is immaterial, right?"

Thousands were nothing compared to hundred million dollar balances.

I nodded. "But it adds up."

"At this point, it could be nothing. Finish the bank confirmations and don't focus on this. The amounts are recorded?" I nodded. "Then let's assume they are verified transfers. Add it to the list of questions we ask when we do the interviews with the staff."

As a part of the audit, we were required to perform short interviews with the staff to verify procedures and separation of duties.

"Fine."

Before I could go in, the damnable man asked again, "The ring?"

I didn't bother to look back and said, "Still looking."

Though he reached for me, I'd slipped inside before he could stop me.

It was later in the day that I received another text which outweighed the **I'm glad** response I'd gotten in response to my **delicious dinner** message. I'd thought that was the end of it. The end of us, not that there had been an us. But the **meet me for dinner, 6pm** text suggested he wasn't.

I got up from my seat and headed for the restroom. Once there, I glanced under the doors to see if I was alone before calling Lizzy.

"Must be important if you are calling me at work," she said.

"He asked me out again."

"Not exactly a shocker."

"It is when he only responded with a **I'm glad** text to my message about dinner last night," I said.

She sighed. "I was afraid of that. We are dealing with a man used to control."

"What do I do?"

It wasn't like I wanted to play games, but I also didn't want to get hurt. Lizzy blew through guys like her heart was made of ice. I'd like to think I was strong, but the truth was, I wasn't.

"What do you want to do?" she asked.

I wanted to lie to myself, but I didn't to her. "I want to go," I admitted.

There were moments when he made me feel like the most desirable woman on the planet. I craved that feeling.

"Then go."

I exhaled once. "Okay, I will."

"Details," she said. "I want lots of details."

After we hung up, I opened his text and responded, **Where?**

I assumed he'd take a little time to get back to me, but before I could put my phone away, it vibrated in my hand.

I'll make a reservation, it read.

My stomach did a little backflip. There was just something about the man that made me want to ignore all the warning bells that I would end up getting hurt.

As I settled back in my seat, it was the million dollars' worth of transfers I couldn't trace back to an invoice or to another bank account that drew me out of my thoughts of Kalen.

Scott looked up from where he sat with his sleeves rolled up. Though the man was handsome, there had never been the kind of pull to him that I felt when I merely thought of Kalen.

At around five, I realized I was too close to something to stop. I sent a quick text to Kalen.

I'm not going to make it.

I waited for the telltale dots to appear that he was responding. When nothing came, I sent another impromptu message.

Dinner at my place at 7 instead?

I felt foolish for staring at the screen like a schoolgirl with a crush.

"Did you find something?"

My heart stopped. I'd been so focused waiting for Kalen's response, I hadn't heard Scott's approach.

Quickly, I put my phone facedown on the conference table in front of me.

"Actually, yes," I began.

I'd found a pattern. The transactions occurred around the same time money was distributed to partners. A lot of money moved during those times.

"I requested more information about the transfers from their accounting team."

Scott's eyes narrowed on me. "You did it without running it by me, after our talk this morning?"

I didn't understand the anger burning in his stare.

"I didn't think it was a problem."

"I'm lead on this audit."

There would surely be blood for how hard I was biting my tongue.

"It's done," I said instead.

"I want to be told immediately when you get that information back."

"Fine." I gritted my teeth, wondering how I'd make it through this assignment with him as my boss. At least he hadn't reminded me again about the stupid ring.

At six-fifteen, I gathered my things. Scott made his way over to me.

"Where are you going?" he asked quietly. "I'm having dinner brought in."

"I have to go," I said emphatically.

"We have a job to do, and that means late nights when necessary."

"I've been here since before six am," I said.

"Yet, you still have more to do. What's the emergency that you have to leave?"

I glared at him. "Are you asking if I have a doctor's appointment? Like with a gynecologist to see if you gave me any STDs while cheating on me."

Perversely, I grinned as his jaw tightened.

"Don't worry. I'll be getting a checkup tonight."

With that, I walked out of the room, feeling like I scored the winning goal. Scott's face had turned beet red.

FOURTEEN

THERE WAS UNDENIABLE SEXUAL CHEMISTRY BETWEEN Kalen and me. Something I recognized as I walked up to my building and caught sight of him stepping out of a black SUV. Embarrassingly, my body readied for him instantly.

Our eyes locked and I swallowed, wondering if I would make it through dinner. This instantaneous need was something I hadn't experienced with any other man.

"Lass," he said, ratcheting up my desire for him.

"Kalen."

Unspoken words bounced between us as we stared at each other.

"I think we should go inside," he said with a grin.

Humiliation colored my cheeks. Had I really just been standing there like a lost puppy?

Gathering some of my composure, I'd repeated his phrase from the other night, trying to regain some control. "Yes. It's cold out."

"Good evening, Miss Glicks," the doorman said as I

strode through the open door like I hadn't been mesmerized by the man following me.

"You too, Stan," I said, turning back to give him a smile.

"It's supposed to snow tonight," he said, eyeing Kalen.

"That's what four-wheel drive is for," Kalen said as if he was annoyed the guy had spoken to me. A hand landed at my back and steered me to the elevator, ending any further conversation. It was as if he was familiar with the building.

"He was being nice," I muttered.

Kalen's only response was a lifted brow.

"What floor?" he asked, ignoring my comment as we stepped into the elevator.

Instead of answering, I pressed it myself and looked up in time to catch his reaction. Then his eyes dropped to my lips. They felt suddenly dry and I let my tongue sweep over them. Realizing what I'd done, I dropped my gaze to avoid his.

That was when I noticed the bag he carried for the first time. "Something smells good," I said in an effort to tamp down the sexual tension.

"It does," he said, prowling forward, and I took an involuntary step back.

Just as I'd been about to mention that I'd planned to cook, the bell dinged. He created some separation between us as the doors opened. A yapping dog broke free of his tiny owner and leaped into the elevator. I bent down and caught him as Kalen steadied the older woman who had been dragged along.

"Are you all right?" he asked her.

The white-haired woman looked at Kalen like he was a god.

"I'm fine thanks to you, young man," she said as he righted her on her feet.

He flashed her that spell-casting grin of his as I held her dog out. She took him from me as Kalen kept the doors open.

"Are you going down?" she asked. When we shook our heads in tandem, she apologized. "I must have pressed the wrong button."

"No problem," he said, that sexy accent of his mesmerizing both of us.

"Too bad," she said, grinning and then winking at him as the doors closed.

"What was that all about?" I asked, amused by Kalen's continued grin.

"She's a pincher."

I stood perplexed for a second. Her hand hadn't reached for his face and my jaw dropped when I put it together.

"She didn't?" I asked.

"She did."

I let loose a laugh. "She pinched your bottom," I said absently, and he nodded.

Seconds later, the elevator came to a stop. I shook my head as I led him down the hall to a door on the right. I fumbled with the keys because the man was too close, and I hadn't texted Lizzy to warn her I was bringing home a guest. I didn't want to give her a show. Though knowing her, she'd be thrilled given her encouragement of late. When she didn't pop her head out, I assumed she wasn't in.

"Nice place," he said as we walked in.

In front of me a mirror hung where I was able to

glimpse him setting the bag down on the island. Then his dark stare landed on me, looking positively predatory.

"This is crashing at a friend's. I'm just an ordinary girl, without the shine." I did a little twirl as I held out my hands to encompass the room and my nerves got to me knowing what was coming. I ended up stumbling over my feet.

Mr. Tall, Dark, and Dangerous caught me before I fell. And holy crap on a cracker. The sexual tension between us hit a feverish pitch, despite my efforts to squash it with truths and quips.

I danced out of his hold, which was a bad thing considering I'd almost fallen once. I smacked right into the wall, which probably knocked some sense into me.

"Hey," he said, suddenly there, probing at my temple while peering into my eyes.

"I'm okay," I said, waving him off and trying my best to keep it together. I resisted searching for a bump on my head myself as the rest of me was still at attention. Rather, still ready for his attention.

"I didn't grow up with the shine either," he said, taking a look around.

I appreciated that he let it go and didn't make a fuss over my clumsiness. I would have been more embarrassed. Instead, I assessed myself and felt fine. I went for two glasses.

Looking over my shoulder, I asked, "Self-made man?" to keep the conversation going.

"Isn't that the only way?" he asked, eating up the distance between us. "Are you sure you're okay? Maybe you should lie down."

I glanced over at the mirror, wondering if I had a growing bruise on my head. But there wasn't one.

"What, are you playing doctor now?" I teased and searched for a bottle of red wine based on the smells coming from the bag he brought.

Suddenly, he was way too close, not allowing me the space I needed to calm my body down. "No, but I'm in the mood to play if you're okay."

He bent over to nip at my neck, and I felt his erection grow at our contact.

Slow your racing heart, I warned myself. I wasn't the creature he was making me out to be. But screw it. I needed this. I wasn't going to fight it. It wasn't like I was a virgin. My parents may not have approved of my behavior. But what did it matter? I never planned to return home—not permanently at least.

"What did you bring for dinner?" I asked, sounding way too breathless.

"Steak, if you're hungry."

Oh, I was hungry, but which hunger was winning out at that moment, I wasn't sure.

"I'm a meat and potatoes kind of girl," I said in jest.

Quirking up an eyebrow, he moved to the island to pull containers out of the bag. It wasn't your ordinary takeout. The food was in an insulated carrier and there was still a little sizzle as he removed things.

I ventured to the cabinets and pulled out plates. Seamlessly, we worked in tandem as if we'd lived together for years. He dished out the food as I gathered silverware and a corkscrew.

By the time we sat down at the island, I still wasn't sure

we'd make it through dinner. My body was a live wire, fully aware of his every movement.

I tried my best to focus on my food, but his kissable lips inspired fantasies I wanted to recreate. I tightened my thighs, trying not to be so affected by him.

"So, are you a restaurateur?" I asked.

When his brow lifted, I added, "You seem adept at picking meals, having them available and delivered with a mere thought."

He chuckled. "No, I don't actually own any restaurants."

"Oh, and here I thought a mere mortal would have said, 'I don't work at a restaurant.' But you said own."

I let him chew on that and thought he might not say anything in response.

"Actually, I don't own anything. Not yet at least."

"Mmm," I teased. "So, does that mean in the future you will?"

An amused smile played on his lips. "That's the plan."

Just as I looked for something to say, he lifted his hand and cupped my chin. I wasn't prepared for him to skim his thumb across my lower lip, over to the corner of my mouth, only to then lick it clean.

"You had a spot there," he said, pointing at my mouth.

There was no way I would let him see my disappointment that he hadn't drawn me in for a kiss. I couldn't remember if we'd ever kissed. But that wasn't true. We hadn't. We'd nipped at each other during the countdown. But that was it.

I stood, picking up my plate. He must have read me well because he followed. When I set my dish in the sink, he came up beside me and did the same before dipping his head low. Only his lips ghosted over mine, their destination farther than I'd wanted.

At my ear, he said, "I have to have you, lass. I can't wait any longer."

Call me weak, but dammit, I was. The pulse at my center was a detonator ready to go off. What did kissing matter? I lied to myself. He's just a fuck buddy, as Lizzy would say.

I gave over to the impulse. "Have me."

With that, he scooped me up and tossed me over his shoulder, sending a shriek out of my mouth. "I'm not a sack of potatoes," I protested in a fit of giggles.

"No, you taste better," he said, walking down the hall like he knew where he was going. Although the apartment was huge, there was only the one hallway. "Which is your room?"

Blood rushed to my head, leaving me a little breathless. Not to mention being so near his ass. I snickered thinking about the old woman who'd pinched it and managed to answer, "Last door on the right."

He went right through and didn't bother to close it. When he set me down, I was positioned facing the wall. He lifted my hands above my head and said, "I can't wait, lass. I've been dying to get inside you all day."

All day? He'd been thinking about me all day. That thought fluttered away in a breeze like floating white puffs from a seeded dandelion when his mouth began to suck at my pulse point.

Kalen was very skilled at the one-hand thing. While

restraining my wrists, he managed to unbutton my pants and have them pooling at my feet in an instant.

"What did I tell you about pants, lass?"

The infuriating man was wasting his breath on the wrong thing.

"It wasn't like I was expecting you," I snapped until his thumb rubbed slightly over the bundle of nerves at my center and I moaned.

"Always expect me," he said, tweaking my nipple. He was so smooth. I barely registered his one hand possessing my body, expertly moving from one erogenous region to the next before sensations filled me. "You're wet for me."

I sighed when a finger slipped inside me.

"Please." I found myself begging and didn't have to ask twice. There was the sound of a zipper and a rip of a square package. Then the breath left my lungs as he filled me completely.

His hands left my wrist. "Keep your hands on the wall above your head."

The command should have grated on my nerves. Instead, it sent a spike of pleasure. He lifted me by my waist like I weighed nothing and let me slide down his length. Heat flooded me, remembering our first night together. I felt boneless, like I was riding a cloud.

"Fuck," he grunted. "So wet."

The pleasure he created in and out of me was without mercy. I longed for something to grip onto as he slammed into me again and again. He was incredibly strong, using one hand to glide from my hip to rub my clit as he continued his assault on my core. My toes barely touched the ground.

"Are you ready?" he asked, sliding his cock over a spot inside me that made my knees weak.

"For what?" I asked.

"This."

His other hand flicked my clit once and then twice. That was all it took to send me flying over the edge like a hang glider as if my body had waited for his silent command. Moments later, he followed me into bliss.

When he steadied me on my feet, I nearly begged for him to stay inside me. Words, however, were like an oasis in a desert. I could see them but couldn't reach them. So we stood, with his body still covering mine, panting out the frenzy that had overcome us. In the ensuing silence, we both heard the front door open.

FIFTEEN

Keys jingled as they hit the granite countertop, creating a sound that reverberated through the apartment. It had to be Lizzy and not Matt, which was a total blessing. Matt would have strolled directly to my open bedroom door and caught me with my pants down, literally.

"Bails, are you home? Is that Matt with you?"

I let my head fall against the wall. It was an automatic response. Oh, how her words had sounded, but there was nothing to do about it now.

"It's me," I called out. "And Matt's not here." I had no choice but to admit that or she might have come to my room and caught me in the act.

"Ooo," she said, sounding full of regret. "I forgot something. I'll be back later." And just as quickly as she'd come, she was gone.

Lizzy deserved the supreme best friend award and I was so grateful she was mine.

Once the door closed, Kalen spun me around. His eyes

had darkened from a forest green to midnight, if that was possible. "Who's Matt? Are you fucking him too?"

In retrospect, I couldn't blame him for coming to that conclusion. But in the moment, I responded with a crashing thwack, slapping him hard across the face. "How dare you?"

His eye blazed and my mouth dropped. I covered it with my hands in the realization that I shouldn't have struck him.

Before I could apologize, he snarled, "What did you expect me to think?"

His anger only fueled mine.

"I expected you to ask and not assume, asshole."

"I did ask." He sounded like he was restraining himself from a reacting to the stinging red mark across his face. It was illuminated by the hall light. We hadn't bothered to turn any others on.

"No, you asked and then made judgments. Matt is my roommate's brother. As I've said before, you are only the third man I've ever slept with. So, despite my recent behavior, I bet I'm Mother Teresa compared to you. Now get the hell out."

When he stepped toward me, I shoved at his chest and felt the coiled muscles tense there. He was like a mountain but didn't press forward. "Lass," he began.

"Don't you lass me. Just lass your way out of my apartment," I said, standing firm but not touching him. Touching him again would be bad. It would be too easy to give in.

His eyes swept the room and remained motionless for a second too long. I followed his line of sight to an unmistakable pair of men's pants and a dress shirt draped over a chair. I closed my eyes, knowing how it looked. My first thought was to explain. But when his murderous gaze landed on me, I held my tongue.

"And I suppose those are Matt's clothes in your room?"

"Yes," I said quickly. "But this is none of your business. You don't own me."

Reaching down, he pulled up his pants and said, "You're right. I don't."

Stepping out of my own pants, because I wasn't going anywhere except to the shower once he was gone, I said, "Don't you dare look at me that way. I was supposed to get married that night when I met you. Instead, I found myself drunk fucking a total stranger."

Invitations had been sent out for that date. Luckily, I learned the truth about my cheating fiancé weeks before I made the mistake of walking down the aisle with Scott.

Fastening his pants, he didn't look like he believed me, and for some reason I wanted to cry. "I just bet," he stated.

"Fuck you," I cried out as he strode out of the room.

"I already did that, sweetheart," he called out in a matter-of-fact kind of way. Because he hadn't called me lass, somehow that hurt even more. Sweetheart wasn't close to sweet coming from his lips. It made me feel more like a slut. And wasn't I one?

When the front door closed, I leaned back on the wall where I'd just had mind-blowing sex with a man who wormed his way under my skin. I slid down said wall as the realization that I wouldn't ever have that again caused my knees to buckle.

SIXTEEN

It took me a long time to peel myself up from the floor. Skid marks from the little makeup I'd worn streaked down my face. I wiped my eyes as if I could remove the evidence of my despair as I stared at the braided ring that should have been a reminder of who I was. I opened a window in my room, despite the chill and headed to the kitchen.

I cleared the table of food and wine, unable to leave a mess for someone else to clean up. Lizzy hadn't returned and it was Matt who walked in. When he caught sight of my face, concern filled his.

"Who do I need to kill?" he asked, with such a deadpan expression I choked out a laugh. Leave it to him to know what to say.

"No one," I said, somewhere between a laugh and a sob.

And wasn't that the truth. Kalen hadn't done anything I hadn't asked him to. His questions were legitimate, albeit crude. Wouldn't I have reacted the same way if the situation had been reversed?

Matt's strong arms wrapped me in a hug anyway.

"I know how to get rid of a body," he whispered, his lips close to my ear.

I coughed out a half-laugh. "Thanks. I'll call you if the need arises."

He didn't let go and said soberly, "If you want to talk about it..."

Did he think I was crying over Scott?

I pulled back and his hand dropped away. I wiped at the corner of my eyes to remove the stray moisture.

"I'm fine, really. It's nothing," I said.

The last thing I was going to do was tell Matt about what happened between Kalen and me.

"Are you sure? I don't want to leave you like this."

I mustered up my best smile.

"Really, I'm good. Sad to see you go. But I'm fine, really."

His grin widened. "Just say the word, darling, and I'm yours."

It was a tempting offer, but the last thing I needed was another man in my life. Besides, the spark that had fueled my crush on him years ago wasn't anything like it used to be.

"You're a good friend," I said instead.

He put a hand to his heart. "Damn, friendzone. It's a cold, cold place."

His amusement freed me from any guilt. Matt may have said he was interested, but he wasn't in love with me either. Not that I expected him to be. I wasn't even sure it was me he wanted or if he finally decided to settle down.

I went in for another hug.

"Safe travels," I murmured.

He squeezed me. "You deserve the best, darling. Don't settle for less." And when he pulled back, his grin was filled with straight white teeth. "And we know who the best is."

I giggled, feeling a lightness in my chest.

"I'm going to be sorry I let you go, aren't I?" I teased.

He pointed at me. "You said it, not me."

When he went to get his bag, I went back to putting away the dishes I'd washed and dried. The apartment felt lonely when he finally left.

I had a moment of regret when the door closed behind him. Matt made me laugh and he was sexy as hell. But the truth was, I wasn't in the right place to take him up on his offer. In too short of time, I'd broken up with my fiancé and slept with a perfect stranger.

A relationship, albeit a long-distance one with my best friend's brother or anyone for that matter, wasn't the right move. The question was, what to do now?

SEVENTEEN

WHEN THE DOOR OPENED, I LOOKED UP FROM WHERE I'd curled up on Lizzy's impossibly white sofa with a mug of coffee in my hand, praying I wouldn't spill a drop. I hadn't been able to go to my room with memories of Kalen still so fresh.

"That smells good," Lizzy said and went for her Nespresso machine.

I could tell she wanted to talk to me as much as I wanted to talk to her.

"So," she said, exhaling a breath.

"So," I said back.

She wanted details, but I had no idea where to begin.

"Matty's gone?" she asked.

I nodded. "Yeah, he left a little while ago."

But then, she took the conversation in a different direction.

"I guess it didn't go how he hoped."

I sucked in a quick intake of breath. "You knew?"

She held my gaze as if to say, *You're kidding me.*

"I had a crush on him for like ever," I said.

"Yeah, I knew that too."

We were silent another moment before I finally said, "Why didn't you say anything?"

Waving an absent hand, she said, "Who wants to talk to their best friend about how hot their brother is? I had enough of that in high school. And I figured the two of you would get together eventually."

"But Scott came along," I added, continuing her thought.

"And, when I saw Scott, I thought for sure Matt would see how you'd picked a guy that looked almost like him." She waited a beat before speaking as if to see if I'd deny it. Looking back, it was probably true. It wasn't that I'd sought a replacement since Matt hadn't been interested. But when Scott came along, I might have subconsciously ignored all the warning bells about him because he did remind me of Matt, physically at least.

"And you stayed with Scott even when I could tell you weren't into him," she said.

"You know about how conservative my family is?" I said. She didn't know all of it. There were just some things that remained secret. "My parents wouldn't have approved of my unmarried sexual relationship with Scott. If they ever found out, I could be... um... I guess the best way to describe it is excommunicated. I would never be allowed home again."

The first time had been a mistake. I was drunk and needy. Scott had been there, right time, right place.

"You had sex, Bails?" she said in mock horror.

"I was raised to believe that sex was reserved for your

husband and no one else. They would see it as me bringing shame to my family. The only way to excuse the behavior is to get married. Somehow in my head, staying with him felt like the compromise between their world and the one I wanted for myself."

I wasn't sure she'd understand, but I'd tried my best to explain.

"By dating him, you validated your decision to take the relationship further?" she asked, but it was more of a statement.

"Exactly," I answered.

"Scott wasn't your first, though."

This she knew. "No. Turner was."

I'd bucked the rules all my life. Though Scott and even Kalen had been an impulse, Turner had been a choice made out of love.

"You grew up with him, right?"

I sipped my coffee, which had started to go lukewarm, then said, "Yes. And if our parents had found out, we would have been married on the spot," as my eyes fell on the only ring I wore.

"You loved him, right?" she asked, drinking from her own mug.

"Yes, I'll always love him," I said, fiddling with the ring. To myself, I added, *in ways*. "I could have survived being married to him."

"Did he give you that?" she asked, her hand landing on my finger. I nodded. "What happened?"

This was a part of the story Lizzy had never pushed before. We were usually too busy talking about her failed relationships and my doomed one to dive deeper.

"I would have eventually married him if I'd stayed," I began.

"Did he give you that ring?"

She stared pointedly at the ring I hadn't been able to take off.

I thought about the day Turner had given me the ring. "Yes."

"Is it an engagement ring? Wait, I thought you said they didn't know about the sex?" she asked, switching gears midstream.

"They didn't. Not then at least. We were paired, or what you might call betrothed, I guess, for lack of a better word. His family and mine had been in discussion about our future marriage. But then, my dad caught us. He assumed Turner would tell his parents and they would see me as a suitable wife. Not the first one at least."

Her eyes widened, reminding me of my father's shock at catching us. His anger had scared me that day.

"First wife?"

I shrugged. "It isn't uncommon for men in our community to take on more than one wife. Though they aren't truly married to the others, as that's not legal."

"Your father?" she asked.

"No, he didn't. More for my mother. He loved her enough not to."

She nodded. "You didn't marry him, though."

Him, being Turner.

"No." I thought for a moment before I spoke. "My mom told me to pursue my dreams and go to college. She didn't want me to get stuck when she got that it wouldn't make me happy. It was the first time I'd been given the option of true freedom. I left him behind because I didn't think he'd be willing to leave. He loved his life there and I loved him enough to not make him choose. His place was there."

"Wow. Where is he now?"

Her question seemed redundant. But I guess in her mind lots of time had passed and possibly things had changed. "He's still there as far as I know. The last time I visited, he was with someone else."

Yet, that knowledge had not gotten me to toss away his ring like how I'd easily done with Scott's. And that ring had been far more valuable than the steel ring Turner had forged for me.

"That was years ago," she said.

"Yes, and I'll admit it hurt knowing he moved on. I couldn't go back after that."

"And then you met Scott."

It was a point I hadn't considered. Matt had been a safe crush because he hadn't been available. Turner seemingly happy with someone else had inadvertently left me vulnerable. Scott was there to take advantage, though he wasn't some sort of predator. It just put things into prospective.

I shook my head. "I was hurt and needed..."

"Physical contact."

I nodded.

"I don't blame you. If I ever saw Mason again, I'm not sure what I'd do."

Mason was Lizzy's first love and first everything, though he turned out to be a grade A asshole. "They stick with you."

They did. Turner being my first love.

Lizzy set her mug down on the coffee table, folded herself in the chair like a pretzel, and changed the subject.

"Did Matty meet Kalen? I assume that's who you were with when I came home earlier."

"How do you do that?" I asked. I was getting off topic, but I couldn't help myself.

"Lots of yoga and don't dodge. Did they face-off?" Her gray eyes penetrated me like she was reading my soul.

"No. And yes Kalen was here," I said with both a smile and a grimace. In all likelihood, I would never see Kalen again.

She looked thoughtful, like she was trying to put something together in her head. "Go on, tell me what happened because I can tell something did."

"We had a fight." I drank the rest of my coffee. I didn't want to blame her for what happened, but I knew once I told her, she was going to feel really bad.

"Because of me?"

"Not exactly." It was the truth.

"But I mentioned Matt."

I nodded.

"I'm sorry, Bails."

"It's okay. You couldn't have guessed."

"Matt told me he was going to talk to you. I assumed you two came to your senses and were having excellent monkey sex."

"Monkey sex?" I asked, eyebrow arched.

She twisted her mouth instead of saying *sure,* long and exaggeratedly.

"You were having monkey sex. Just not with Matty?" she asked.

I sighed and told her the story. All of it.

"Man, I'm jealous," she said wistfully. I tossed a throw pillow at her. She giggled and then sobered quickly. "I know this was my fault, but I can't help but say you can't blame him."

Groaning, I said, "I know. But it pisses me off that he didn't even give me a chance to explain. He just judged me and walked out." I looked up at the ceiling, hoping I wouldn't cry.

"Is this pride, or do you really like him?" she asked.

Thinking about it for a second, I said, "Both."

Nodding, she added, "I think he'll be back."

And just like that, my phone chimed from inside my purse. Lizzy smirked like she was psychic and said, "Speak of the devil."

EIGHTEEN

Scott's name flashed on my screen and I hesitated. When I reminded myself he was my current supervisor, I answered.

"Hello," I said.

"Bailey," he slurred.

"Why are you calling?" I asked, holding on to patience as best I could.

"You can keep the ring and come back to me. You might not be the best lay, but you would be a good mother to our children."

I probably should have hung up. Instead, I stated the obvious. "You're drunk."

"Maybe. I miss you," he said.

I reflected on my own feelings and found only disgust.

"Please don't—"

Before I could tell him to delete me out of his contacts, he cut me off.

"I miss your cooking and, damn, if you didn't keep a

clean house. You'd make the perfect wife. Sex isn't every-thing. Maybe we could come to an arrangement."

Old insecurities tried to creep up as I remembered his little comments here and there that had made me feel as though I wasn't good enough for him. That he'd been doing a favor by being with me. That idea had held me in a rela-tionship that hadn't brought me happiness.

"There's no we, Scott," I said with distinct mockery. "It's over. Don't call me again."

I hung up and let out a quick exhale of breath.

Lizzy's eyebrows rose as if she'd overheard Scott's drunken ramble.

"What an asshole," she muttered.

I stood, reminded that maybe if I gave him that damn ring back, he'd stop bothering me and keep things professional.

"Where are you going?" she asked.

"To find his ring."

"You don't have to give it back. He broke the engagement."

That wasn't exactly true. "No, he broke my heart. I broke the engagement."

It wasn't like I had much in the way of jewelry. Most of which Scott had given me over the course of our relation-ship. I considered handing all of it over. I didn't need the reminder.

I found the ring in the small jewelry box underneath everything. It was a simple diamond, not too big and not too small. I remembered how he made a point to show everyone we encountered, making me feel uncomfortable. But that was Scott. Status was important to him. Based on our phone conversation, he'd practically admitted it himself. I was just another object in the life he wanted. How could I have been so stupid?

Lizzy found me staring at it. I looked up as she leaned on the door jam.

"I was never impressed with it," she said.

I closed a fist around it.

"That's because it's simple."

"No," she said, shaking her head. "It wasn't like he put a lot of thought in it. He bought a ring he thought you should have and not what you might have wanted."

That was true. "Now he can give it to his new fiancée."

"And you can screw your brains out with the hot Scot."

A chortle escaped me. I couldn't help it. "Hot Scot."

She nodded. "Got to love alliteration, right? Scott versus Scot. One a bad lay and the other a Scottish dream."

"More like a nightmare versus a fantasy I'll never have again."

"Give him time. He'll be back. Mark my words."

I found my purse and tucked the ring in the zipper pocket so I wouldn't forget it. Then I faced my friend again.

"It's probably for the best. I'm not cut out for the casual thing. One argument and I'm falling to pieces over a guy I barely know."

"Minor setback. Trust me. Give it another chance. You need to get Scott and your parents out of your head. Sexual freedom and all that. Besides, don't you need a date for your company holiday party? Can you imagine the look on Scott's face if you brought Kalen?"

The *holiday party*. How had I forgotten? It was scheduled right after the holidays and before the craziness of audit and tax season took hold.

"I won't go," I said.

Lizzy crossed her arms over her chest and gave me a pointed look.

"Why give Scott the satisfaction of thinking you're too upset over him to show?"

"Why would he think that?" I asked, my fist balling as I thought about his girlfriend's smug reaction if I showed up alone.

"The man's ego knows no bounds. He called, expecting you to marry him while he screwed other women on the side."

She'd heard.

"Not going is better than showing up alone, because Kalen's not an option. And Matt's gone."

I wouldn't ask him to come back to escort me this weekend. Being a cop wasn't a nine-to-five job.

"You could call him," she suggested.

"Who? Matt?"

"No, silly. Mr. Stud."

I blew out a breath. "Sure. I'll just tell him that even though he's a bastard he can take me to my company's holiday party."

She laughed. "Why not?"

I lifted a finger to count off all the reasons why.

"One—he's not interested in dating me. Not that I am, the ass. Two—he'll think I'm trying to back him into more of a relationship. Three—I can see myself mistaking great sex for something more, which brings me back to one and two."

She caught my shoulders slumping and came in for the hug.

"Fine. I'll be your date. That will surely confuse the hell out of Scott."

I laughed. "God, I love you."

"I love you too. Maybe one day we'll both find Mr. Right."

"Maybe," I said.

When she left, I had nothing but my thoughts to keep me occupied. Which led to fitful sleep where fantasies about Kalen's mouth and all the things it could do kept me up half the night. The damnable man wouldn't stay out of my thoughts or my dreams.

NINETEEN

KALEN

THE FIGURES ON THE COMPUTER SCREEN MEANT nothing as I replayed the events of last night in my head.

When my brother strolled through the door, I took a quick glance at my Patek Philippe.

"Isn't it a little early?" I asked Connor.

He stood in black leather pants and a black tee, and probably hadn't gone home from the night before.

"No one ignores the great man when he summons you for a family meeting," Connor said.

I too had gotten the message about the family meeting.

"You too?" he questioned with a raised brow. I shrugged. "What have you done?" Connor asked as if it was a foregone conclusion it was all my fault.

"I'm trying to save this company," I said. "What have you heard?"

He shrugged. "Dad didn't give a lot of details."

"The old man doesn't trust me." As well he shouldn't. I was working for one reason only. Payback. I would never forgive him for what he put my mother through.

"He doesn't trust anyone, including me," Connor said.

Despite my baby brother's dual degrees in business and law, he wanted nothing to do with the company our father had built.

Connor waved me off. "You could always screw your way out of this."

I shook my head and ignored his sexual proclivities. "Not interested in bedding the enemy. You can if you want. Though Father might disown you if you reveal yourself to the public."

He rolled his eyes. "I'm surprised we haven't been outed yet."

I wanted to believe our father had our best interest at heart. More likely, he didn't want to share the limelight. His rules dictated that we use a driver and private elevator that took us directly to our floor when coming into the office. Everyone who worked directly for us was required to sign an ironclad non-disclosure agreement. He was so paranoid, meetings were held on the other side of the building away from our offices.

When I didn't respond to Connor, he said, "You need to get laid. You're too tense."

Though I loathed to admit it even to myself, I couldn't keep my mind off of one smart-mouthed redhead.

I'd known she was trouble when she'd walked into the New Year's Eve party. Never in my life had I been so single-mindedly focused on one woman. I'd tried my best to ignore her presence until a tall guy headed in her direction on the dance floor. That was when I made my move. A primal urge to mark her as mine had overcome me.

Lucky for the guy, he'd gone for the gorgeous but way

too skinny blonde who danced next to her. A mistake on his part. The redhead had the face of an angel and a body the devil himself would pray for. As it turned out, she'd been the sin that tasted like heaven I couldn't forget.

Though I'd been balls deep in her four times, it wasn't enough. Watching her eyes go unfocused as she came had become my drug of choice. But it was her mouth that would be my undoing. Those damn lips of hers had been a temptation, but I wouldn't make that mistake again. If only I could get her off my mind. A bed perhaps. Maybe one time in a bed, all night, of course, would be enough.

Then again, she'd probably never let me touch her again. Finding Matt's clothes in her room had made me see red as if I had a right. The emotion had been so foreign, I hadn't been able to stop the outburst that likely killed any chance of tasting heaven again.

"Bro."

The impatient word had come from a far place and snapped me out of my head. I looked up and saw my brother eyeing me quizzically.

We were of two different minds. Where I'd grown up with three goals. One—to survive the streets. Two—to be rich and never want for anything again. Three—to take my father down several pegs. My brother, on the other hand, had grown up with everything, but wanted none of it.

"How's—" Connor began.

His question was cut off when our dad's pinched-face admin walked in like she owned the place.

"He's ready for you," she announced, eyeing Connor's rock star attire disapprovingly.

I stood, knowing exactly what this meeting was about.

What had he found out? I shook off that thought. Good thing, I already had an explanation ready. There was nothing our father could say that would rattle me. I was fully prepared for anything that came out of the old man's mouth.

TWENTY

BAILEY

I walked into the conference room that morning on a mission. After setting my stuff down, Anna, the only other person in the room, ambushed me.

"I think I saw the Money Man."

I'd been so focused on giving Scott his ring back and setting a course for a new future for myself, I'd completely forgotten about the enigmatic man everyone was speculating about.

When I didn't react quickly enough, she said, "You know who I'm talking about."

I nodded. "How do you know it was him?"

"I mean, I don't know exactly. It wasn't like the person with him said, 'How's your morning, Money Man?'"

I laughed. "True, but why do you think it was him?"

"The person called him Mr. King. And he wasn't an old guy."

My jaw slackened as my fascination increased. "What'd he look like?"

"You know what they say, tall, dark, and handsome. Like totally hot—sunburn levels."

Our conversation was cut short when the guys walked in. Anna guiltily slunk away. If they'd been paying attention, she so would have given away that we'd been talking about something other than work.

I sat and turned my computer on as Scott hadn't arrived. I was deep into tying out bank numbers when he showed up two hours later.

"Status update," he said and proceeded to talk to each of us individually.

I took the ring out of my purse and gripped it tightly. Though Lizzy had several colorful ideas what I should do with the ring, including handing Scott a pawn slip, those were lost to me. Scott had made a point to send me a text about New York and Massachusetts laws which required me to return the ring; effectively stopping me from doing anything creative with it.

When he got to me, the first thing I did was discreetly put the ring in his hand.

"I hope you choke on it," I said quietly and took satisfaction from his eyes bugging out before launching into my update about the missing money in the bank accounts.

"Have you heard from their accounting team?" he asked professionally, having recovered from my earlier comment.

"Not yet."

"Well, let me know when you do."

He closed a hand around the ring and walked away with no mention of his ludicrous call the night before.

Late that evening as I was packing up, my phone buzzed. Pulling it out, I saw it was an unknown caller.

I put it to my ear and quietly said, "Hello," after accepting the call.

"Lass," a rough, masculine voice said. He was breathing heavy and I wondered what exactly he was doing. Incidentally, I was also grateful he used the endearment "lass" and not "sweetheart".

Quickly, I stepped out of the room, making a beeline for the bathroom, and asked, "Why is your number blocked?"

Nervous tension had coursed through me at what he potentially might say. Automatically I'd gone on the defensive, throwing out a question to keep him off balance.

"It's always been that way," he said matter-of-factly.

I closed myself in a stall and leaned on the wall, reminded how we'd spent our first time together.

"The other night," he began.

"Was a mistake," I quickly said. When his silence became too much, I rushed to say more. "You were an ass, but I shouldn't have slapped you."

All I got in response was his breathing, which got increasingly louder over muffled conversations in the background. "Where are you?" I asked.

It was a second before he said, "In the gym."

That fit with the sounds I heard. Which begged the question as to why was he calling me?

He didn't sound drunk or seem like the type. "What are you doing?" I asked, wondering why I was the one taking the lead in this conversation.

"Using a punching bag to forget about you," he said.

Okay. I wanted to be pissed off by his response, but his voice was like lava, burning me inside and out. "Calling me probably isn't helping," I tossed out.

"Just tell me one thing. Is this Matt guy your fiancé?"

"No," I said, quickly looking up at the ceiling. I should probably apologize for that, but I found that I couldn't. "Now that that's cleared up, I'll let you get back to working hard to forget me."

My finger hovered to end the call when he spoke. "I need to see you tonight."

"No," I asserted.

"We both handled last night badly," he retorted. Several rapid thumping sounds came through the line. I imagined him sexily dripping with sweat as he circled a punching bag.

"True, but seeing you will only lead to sex, and you don't hold me in high regard in that area."

The word "sex" combined with his rough breathing were doing a number on my underwear.

"It's none of my business what you do," he said.

I laughed, flattening myself to the wall, and covered my head with my forearm. "You already passed judgment on me. I'm surprised I'm not in your cast out pile."

"Me too."

My mouth opened, and then I paused before flatly stating, "Goodnight, Kalen," in response to his thoughtless comment.

"Wait," he said, and I paused, though I should have just hung up. "Let me take you out to dinner?"

Shaking my head, even though he couldn't see, I said, "No." And I ended the call. Not wanting to be tempted by answering if he called back, I put my phone on silent, not vibrate.

I went back to the conference room, grabbed my things,

and headed home. After a hot shower, I sat on the sofa, prepared to find a movie that wasn't romance-based to pass the time until Lizzy got home.

A banging noise startled me awake. Flustered that I hadn't realized I'd fallen sleep, I fluttered my eyes open. As I tried to figure out if the noise was real or a remnant of my dream, another knock came and truly woke me up.

I went to the door and peered through the peephole. There he was, all six-feet-three, maybe four, of solid Scottish man. From what I could see, he wore jeans and a sweater that clung to his muscled chest. He looked around like he expected to see something or someone else.

And that just pissed me off. Frowning, I swung the door open and said, "Why are you here?"

TWENTY-ONE

HE WASN'T AT ALL INTIMIDATED BY THE GLARE I'D thrown his way. Promptly, he stepped in and closed the door, forcing me to take several steps back. His stalking forced a hitch in my breath as my pulse raced. My body immediately came alive.

"You don't want me," I weakly protested. It was one thing to make a stand over the phone. It was another to try that in the flesh.

He stepped closer to me and took my hand, pressing it against his solid erection. My mouth went wide, partly in protest and partly in desire.

"My cock says otherwise," he answered, responding to my *you don't want me* statement.

Feeling the moisture grow between my legs, I snatched my hand away and managed to say, "I can't do this. I'm not the kind of woman that does casual relationships."

"I'm not the kind of man that thinks about a woman twice after I've had her," he said.

"That proves my point. This isn't going to work."

"Yet, I've had a hard-on since I heard your voice today and it's not going away. I have the worst fucking case of blue balls. I can't think except about being deep inside you."

"And that's supposed to be romantic?" I asked, looking up at him.

"I can't help that I'm sexually attracted to you any more than you can help wanting me."

I wished he was exaggerating.

"That doesn't solve anything," I said, folding my arms, afraid I might reach out and touch him.

"We can come to a compromise," he began. "Neither of us wants a relationship."

"Agreed," I said stubbornly, though it was the truth.

"You don't want a fuck buddy and I don't want a girl-friend. We can meet each other halfway."

I thought about Lizzy. She'd be laughing her ass off if she caught wind of this conversation.

"How so?" I asked, hoping his answer would piss me off enough I could tell him to leave instead of desperately wanting to screw his brains out. That feeling of desperation he gave to me was still foreign and confused me about how I should feel.

"I can give you exclusivity."

"How is that not a relationship?" I asked.

"You'll be the only woman I'll be with until we can get out of each other's head."

Though I didn't necessarily agree, I nodded, mulling over his offer.

"Basically a fuck buddy," I said, hating the phrase.

"Not exactly. I won't be thinking about other women. I

have little time to spare in the day. During those times, I can be with you."

It felt like a set up to disaster, and I thought of one thing that would get him to give up on the idea because I couldn't find the words to say no. Damn him for making me weak.

"One caveat. I need a date for my company's holiday party this coming Saturday."

"A date," he said, brow arching perfectly.

I shook my head. "Not a date. An escort."

"Why do you need a date?"

"Not a date. An escort," I repeated, feeling the heat in my cheeks. "And I don't need one. But you'd be doing me a favor."

"A favor how?"

He was going to make me spell it out, so I blurted, "My ex will be there."

"The one you were going to marry?"

I silently agreed with a curt bob of my head.

"Do you want to make him jealous?"

A bubble of laughter escaped me. "No." I shook my head. "Not a chance."

"Then what?"

I blew out a breath. "My hope is that if he sees me with someone else, he'll have no choice but to accept that I've moved on."

That wasn't the only reason. Seeing his reaction would be a bonus.

"What time?"

Oh crap, was he agreeing?

"Six, it's a black-tie event."

He nodded. "Okay."

"What does that mean?" I asked, even though I knew I'd gotten my terms from the devil himself if his grin was any indicator.

"It means when I want to fuck, I call you and you do the same. But if neither of us is available, we don't get jealous or question the whys. And we won't screw anyone else until our arrangement is over. Agreed?"

He held out a hand.

What was I doing? I reached out mine. "Agreed."

But he didn't take my hand. He reached for the sash on my robe and tugged it open. I wore a tank top and underwear as I'd been too lazy to put on anything warmer than the robe.

"And what are you going to do about my blue balls?" All the talk about his rock-hard dick had my eyes wandering downward. "You see something you like?" he asked cockily.

Flushing, I used my free hand to cover my face. There was just nowhere to look. He pulled my hand free from my face, his eyes hot on mine. He didn't let go, only led me back to my bedroom where all traces of Matt were gone. I didn't object and found myself sitting on the side of my bed, staring directly at his very large erection.

"Unzip my pants," he commanded.

Not lifting my head completely, I looked up at him with only my eyes, knowing my face was filled with contempt.

"Do you always order your partners around?" I asked.

His hand took a fist full of my hair and tugged back, firmly but not roughly. A gasp left my parted lips. Then his other hand reached down to cup my breast, kneading my nipple. "Does it turn you on?"

Not wanting to be easy prey, I just stared at him.

"If you don't want to, I could always leave. No games," he announced. And like that, his hands left my hair and my breast.

I was both pleased and pissed at the same time. Pleased he'd gotten the message. Pissed because he was right. I wanted this. It was foolish of me to think I could ignore this man.

Our chemistry spoke to each other on a molecular level. So maybe that was all we had. Why shouldn't I enjoy this part of me? God only knew if another man would ever make me feel this way. At least we were honest about what we wanted. No games, like he said.

My hand made quick work on the fly of his jeans, and I realized he was once again commando underneath. I pushed his pants down to his knees. I'd trapped him in a sense, but with my legs on either side of him, I was also open to him in a way.

"Take me in that saucy mouth of yours."

His sexy brogue was the cherry on top of the sundae. I tasted him, fully aware that I was submitting to his will. When he groaned and again fisted a hand in my hair, almost to the point of pain, I took him all the way to the back of my throat.

I may have been inexperienced in terms of the number of men I'd slept with, but I wasn't inexperienced with the act itself. Scott had taken pride in teaching me exactly what he wanted. But with him, it was a chore. I did it mostly when I was on my period and he'd complain about how much he needed to get off. And according to Scott logic, we were going to get married anyway. So how could it be wrong?

This was different. I wanted this probably as much as Kalen did. I sucked his length up and down, keeping the pressure of my lips firm but the inside of my mouth hollow enough, working not to graze him too much with my teeth.

"Fuck," he said, his voice cracking. Hearing him begin to come apart and enjoy what I was doing made me feel powerful, even though I'd given in to him. My own orgasm was building. Which was crazy because the only hand he had on me was in my hair at this point. I swirled my tongue on his cock while keeping my mouth around him. He guided his cock with quicker strokes in and out of my mouth. I sucked, I hummed, I licked and sucked again.

"I'm going to come," he murmured.

The moment of truth had *come* in more ways than one. With Scott, I'd always pulled away and used my hand to finish him off. But I wanted this. I wanted to taste Kalen. I moaned around him and cupped his balls, stroking them lightly. A growl preceded his seed shooting down the back of my throat. I stared up at him as he pulsed inside my mouth. His eyes closed in rapture and I took in all his beauty.

Tenderly, he let go of my hair and placed his hand on my cheek. Pulling back, he freed himself from the depths of my mouth. Then he kneeled before me, making us eye to eye a second before he lightly pressed my shoulders to guide me flat on my back. Then he pulled my ass to the edge of the bed and got to his knees on the floor in front of me.

When my eyes widened, he said, "Now it's my turn to feast on you."

It was but a moment before all reason left me. His tongue was wicked in the best way. When his mouth closed over my clit, my back arched, and I knew it wouldn't take much to get me to the finish line.

I'd practically gotten off just by giving him head. His tongue moved expertly, swirling, plunging, tasting until the sheets were fisted in my hands as I thrashed about. When he added a finger or two in the most expert way, I was undone. He found that spot inside me, stroking it while gently biting my clit. I screamed out his name as I came apart. For good measure, he inserted another finger in and out as I rode it all the way through the ecstasy into breathlessness.

My eyes were closed when he flipped me onto my stomach, my feet on the floor as he lifted my ass higher in the air.

"You taste as good as you look." I might have smiled from sheer delight when he added, "I may never get enough."

TWENTY-TWO

Stretching like a cat, I felt limber from another great round of sex. Kalen hadn't ended the night with just his amazing oral skills. He'd bent me over to hold the edge of the bed as he'd sheathed his length inside me like it had always belonged there as he stood behind me.

Tingling sensations of pleasure preceded another amazing orgasm. For the millionth time, I questioned how I would survive our arrangement.

My smile vanished into a frown when I shot up in bed. *Kalen.*

I looked around, noticing he wasn't there. He'd positioned me on the bed when I couldn't stand any longer. Had he left after?

There wasn't any evidence that Kalen was there or had left a note. What was protocol? We hadn't covered that. I glanced at my phone and snatched it up. Using my free hand to push back my unruly hair, I checked for messages. There was an unopened text from his email account.

I clicked it. **I left you a note on your computer.**

From the look of my messenger bag on the floor next to my desk, it didn't appear to have been touched. And how could he have gotten through the security passwords on my work-issued computer anyway?

My eyes drifted to my desk, where my personal MacBook was open just where I'd left it. I moved like a gazelle fleeing from incoming predators. I only had to tap a key to bring my computer to life. I'd disabled the security feature, so it had no password. Maybe I should rethink that. When the screen lit up, a Word document was open.

Lass,

It pains me to leave the warmth of your beautiful body. I'm sorry for it. I would have written you a note, but I couldn't find paper. I didn't want to wake you, so I opted to leave you a note here.

I'll call you or you me. Here is my number.

Kalen

The first thing I did was program his number into my phone. Then I texted him. Something about last night had freed me. If I was going to fuck this man, I wouldn't be ashamed of it.

ME: Cold and lonely over here. I guess I'll have to take a hot shower and think of you while I wash off the scent of you from my skin.

About to put my phone down, I stopped when it emitted a sound that let me know I had an incoming text.

HIM: I'm in a meeting and you've made me hard as stone. I won't be able to get up and shake hands with my business partners when this meeting is over in a few minutes.

Giggling, I decided to tease him some more.

ME: I'll be thinking about that when I hook garters to my thigh-highs under the skirt I wear to work.

I waited a beat for his response and was about to give up when it came through.

HIM: See what you've done to me.

A picture was attached. It was of his lap with a serious tent in his pants. My God, the man was blessed. I still questioned how I'd gotten the whole thing in my mouth.

ME: My my my, Mr. Brinner. Seems like you have quite the problem. I, myself, am heading into the shower with that picture in my mind as I take care of my own problem. Bye.

Quickly, I set the phone down and indeed went to take a shower. I'd be late if I kept sexting Kalen. Besides, he was in a meeting and it wasn't even seven in the morning yet. And honestly, who was this girl I'd become? I'd heard other girls in college, including Lizzy, talk about how they sexted guys. I hadn't understood the concept even when I was with Scott. Maybe because I hadn't been sexually satisfied, but I so got it now and it made me smile.

Dressed and ready for the day, I got my purse and bag before getting my phone. On the way out, I noticed that Lizzy must have either been asleep or not home. Not wanting to wake her in the case of the former, I quietly headed out. In the elevator, I checked my phone and I did, in fact, have a message from Kalen.

HIM: I don't think I can wait until Saturday

to see you. What are your plans for Friday night?

Using both hands, I typed him back. **I can't Friday. I'm going to Lizzy's art showing at her gallery. But tonight I'm free.**

When he didn't respond right away, I headed into the subway to go to work. By the time I'd gotten there, Kalen responded that he had a previous engagement and couldn't. I tried not to think too hard about that. He'd said I would be the only woman he'd be sleeping with, yet for the first time I wondered if he had a wife.

I could have asked but hadn't. Before we ended our back and forth, he'd promised I'd pay for all my teasing when he saw me Saturday. I rode the smile our banter had given me throughout my day as I continued my work reviewing cash accounts.

Later, when I handed the accounting clerk another list of transactions I wanted to review, I saw a flicker of annoyance in his eyes. I was used to it by then. But there was something else. I'd yet to receive anything about my last couple of requests. Something was up and I hated that I would need to discuss it with Scott.

"When do you think you can get me this information?" I asked.

The guy's eyes burned with hate. He huffed, stood up, and said, "Some of these are handled by our international offices. We just consolidate those accounts on our books. It may take a few more days."

I nodded and he strode out of the room. Anna peeked up over her laptop. "What was that about?"

Shrugging, I said, "The usual." You needed thick skin as an auditor, because we were regarded as the enemy. Anna left things at that and Jim barely glanced our way.

By the end of the day I was exhausted and planned to head straight home when the receptionist stopped me.

She waved at me with a small brown envelope.

"This came for you," she said.

As I was required to check in, she knew my name. I took the envelope but didn't open it. It had to be work-related and I was off the clock. I wanted to shut off my brain and veg for a while. I stuffed the envelope into my bag, deciding to deal with it in the morning.

I walked into the apartment to find Lizzy dressed for a night on the town.

"Where are you going, butterfly?" I teased.

"Date," she said.

She'd been seeing the guy she'd met the night I met Kalen.

"I have to say, you sure have been spending a lot of time with this model." I gave her a knowing stare. He wasn't her normal type of rougher around the edges.

"I'm trying something new. You know, Matt's been giving my parents heartburn, especially when he didn't go see them when he came into town. Mom is just devastated." I saw Lizzy's pain for her parents. "He'd asked Mom to meet him for lunch without Dad and she refused. I don't know, Bails." She sighed. "I guess I'm trying to be the good daughter for once."

She had it wrong. From what I could tell, Lizzy was always good to her parents, except when it came to who she dated.

"And how long will that last?" I teased, trying to lighten the mood.

"Who knows," she said. "But he's fun and he's always taking me to all of these industry events. I see the most interesting people. The other day I saw," and she rattled off the names of a few celebrities known to live in New York. "Anyways, though he's not a ton of fun in the sack, we can work on that." She shrugged. If I'd still been with Scott, I might have understood. But I'd seen the light. I wasn't sure I could stay with someone forever anymore and not have great sex.

"So why stay with him?" I asked, peeking out from my search in the refrigerator.

"Oh honey, all men can be taught. He may not be a natural, but I'll still get mine." And she winked.

Shaking my head, I went back to foraging for food. I had to admire her frankness.

"Well, I'm off. You can scream your head off without notice from me tonight," she said, winking again for good measure. Clearly, she'd heard me last night.

The ache between my legs was further evidence of Kalen being there. But tonight, I was on my own. I ate a salad while reading my latest historical novel. This one featured a cover of a sexy Highlander in a kilt holding a sword. I couldn't help imagining Kalen in one. The hero was in the middle of ravaging his woman when my phone rang.

Setting the book down, I answered with a "Hello." I knew it was Kalen because it said unknown caller on the display. It didn't seem to matter that I'd programmed his number in; the privacy feature didn't register it.

When there was no response, I said, "Hello" again. After another soundless second, I hung up.

I almost called Kalen back. Very few people had my number outside of work—Lizzy, Matt, Scott, and Kalen. And only one of them had an unregistered phone number.

Kalen.

Thoughts that he might have a wife, or a significant other, invaded my thoughts. Nothing else made sense. She'd probably checked his phone like I had Scott's and she'd been bold enough to call the number.

Hurt cramped in my gut. Although I held the tears inside, all the feelings of foolishness that I had unwisely trusted Scott came roiling back in. The salad I'd eaten threatened to come back up.

I went into my room, and tried to sleep as I convinced myself I was overreacting. I would give Kalen the chance to answer the question before I drew any more conclusions.

TWENTY-THREE

Lack of sleep over the last several days was my excuse for having overslept. I made it into the office five minutes before Scott showed up. I was reaching into my bag when I noticed the small brown envelope I'd forgotten from the night before. Curious, I opened it and immediately frowned.

Unfolding the single sheet of white paper revealed a short note that read *stop what you're doing*. I read it again before refolding it.

Who the devil, I thought until two likely suspects who could be culpable for the note popped in my head. Based on the scripted handwriting that was suspiciously feminine was the clue. Scott's new fiancée if she'd overheard his drunken confession to me or Kalen's wife. The latter seemed ridiculous. Even if he were involved with someone, how would she have found where I worked? The obvious conclusion was Scott's girlfriend.

As calmly as I could, I said, "Scott, can I speak with

you?" I got up from my seat and he followed me out of the room.

"Look, I don't know what's going on with you and Marisa—"

"Melissa," he corrected.

I waved a hand. "Whatever her name is you set things straight with her. We are not getting back together, so she doesn't need to send me threatening notes. You'd think now that she has the ring, she'd feel secure." I narrowed my eyes at him. "You have given her the ring?"

He ignored that and asked, "Threatening note?"

The jerk looked utterly confused. Not that I would expect more. He still didn't get why I left him for cheating on me. I let go of the question about the ring. It was none of my business.

Instead, I held the note up near his nose so he could read it. He snatched it from my hands and balled it in a fist.

"I'll talk to her."

"Good," I said and went back into the conference room.

The rest of the team busied themselves as if they hadn't been watching us through the glass panes of the conference room walls. I sat and took out my laptop.

Thankfully, work kept me extremely busy. I had a spreadsheet a mile long with the questionable transactions, including amounts coded as bank fees that weren't labeled that way on the bank statements. There was most likely fraud going on at King Enterprises as some had suspected.

After discussing with Scott that I wasn't making headway in getting the information I needed from the King's accounting department, I shut my computer at six on the dot, much to Scott's dismay. But tonight was Lizzy's night and I rushed home to give her all the moral support for her first big event.

"Are you excited?" I asked, rushing through the apartment to stop at her open bedroom door.

She was already dressed impeccably for the showing at her gallery that night.

In reply, she lifted her hands in the air.

"Let's get this party started. And don't you dare bail on me early. We're going for drinks afterwards." She gave her hips a little shake.

"And where is your supermodel?" I responded, smiling.

She waved her already outstretched hands and said, "He had another thing tonight he had to go to. In the biz, it's all about appearances."

Amused, I shook my head and made my way to my room to get ready. We would meet there as she had to leave early to make sure everything was in place.

I thought about Kalen and how I hadn't heard from him. I really wanted to ask him about a wife, but thought it best if I did that in person.

By the time I arrived fashionably late to Lizzy's gallery, the place was packed. It paid to know people like Lizzy and her family did.

Everything was bright with white walls, light bamboo flooring, and colorful art that hung from the rafters to stand on its own and create a maze. Overhead, the place reminded me of a warehouse with exposed beams and pipes, painted so it was clear that they were meant to be seen.

I walked each corridor, naturally progressing to the next. Lizzy had an eye for design. Originally, she had gone to school for that, but her parents steered her toward an art history degree.

Yet, fresh out of college—instead of being someone's assistant, she was her own boss. She certainly had an eye for art. Hell, her apartment looked like an ad in a home and garden magazine.

"Lizzy, this is great," I said, giving her hand a quick squeeze when I caught up to her.

"I know," she said with hushed excitement. "The portraits are selling like crazy. Haven might be an up-and-comer, but she is making a name for herself. I was so lucky to snag her."

Haven was an artist from Chicago, though she'd lived in New York for a while. Matt had recommended Lizzy get in touch with her.

"She's over there."

Haven was stunning as was her companion. Talk about delicious. "And there's a story there. They say he's a priest." When my eyebrow arched quizzically, Lizzy shrugged and added, "Or used to be."

We were interrupted when a regal couple stopped to congratulate Lizzy. When they walked away, Lizzy pulled me in another direction.

"Everything is great." I looked from side to side at the visually interesting art. Then she pointed directly ahead of us. "Except that," I said, when we stopped in front of it. Although it was alone where it sat on the wall, it just didn't fit with all the other pieces.

Her giggle was infectious, and I did too. "Yeah, it was a favor of a favor. You know how things go. Mother's friend had a son or daughter, I can't remember who, wanted to show their art. I couldn't say no, though I'm confused by it as well. But you never know when you might need a favor," she said when our amusement died down.

I was still staring when she said, "You don't mind if I leave you for a bit and attend to my guests?"

"Of course not. Go, I'll be fine," I said. Somehow, I was transfixed by the odd painting, trying to figure it out.

She nodded to me before heading off, looking tall, sleek, and statuesque in a stark white asymmetrical off-the-shoulder sheath. I wasn't a jealous person by nature, but looking at Lizzy, I admired her height and beauty. I felt a little underdressed in the raspberry belted-at-the-waist number I wore, which shouldn't work with my hair color but did. I wasn't expecting to know anyone, but in the back of my mind, I thought of Kalen. I still wanted to see him despite all the questions I had in my head.

After she disappeared, I turned back to the painting. It was tucked in the darkened corner with low light, as if it hoped not to be noticed by anyone. I often felt the same way. I wondered how long I could look at this picture until somebody questioned if I was a crazy person to stare at it.

The background of it was a robin's egg blue. A red blob took up most of the canvas space, as if it were coming at you from the right corner. It didn't create a full circle, leaving me to wonder exactly what the blob was. What was shown and not shown off the canvas, so to speak, was the beginning of a round something. A ball, maybe?

I nearly jumped out of my skin when strong arms came around me. "Don't move." I'd know that brogue anywhere. Some things, however, were instinctual. My head began to swivel to look at him when he cupped my breast and pinched my nipple through the dress. I let out a breath. The pain was sharp but gone as quickly as it had come. "I said, don't move."

Had anyone seen us?

"Kalen," I breathed. His name now came so easily and naturally off my tongue, like it belonged there. "You're here."

"I was invited."

His response was strange. When had he spoken to Lizzy? Then again, he'd left mysteriously in the night. Had they crossed paths in the night? But why wouldn't she mention it?

"Now I told you that you would pay for teasing me." He pressed into my back and the long, hard length of him was apparent.

I could see guests wandering around the place in my peripheral vision. "What are you going to do?" I asked, a little timidly but excited all the same.

"I'm dying to taste you again." I sucked in a breath at his words. Any thoughts of an interrogation into his personal life were gone.

My dress was made of molded material, the kind that was meant to hug the body and not blow in a breeze. If he lifted it in any way, the rest of it was coming along for the ride.

Determined, he leaned in like he planned to whisper in my ear, or so it must have appeared to prying passersby. They would assume we were studying the red blob. I waited. Heck, I was curious to see just what he was going to do. The idea of getting caught was a bit thrilling.

His finger caught the front hem of my dress in the

middle and tugged upwards. I could feel the rest of my dress dragging along. Maybe not at the same pace, but it was riding up as well. I thought for sure he would stop. Lizzy would kill me if I made a spectacle of myself.

"Don't worry. Like at the restaurant, no one can see you behind me, and this time you've been a good girl and wore a dress."

His legs must have been closed tight so nobody could see past him. He definitely dwarfed me. Still, I was ready to protest when his finger grazed my center.

My eyes rolled back, and I felt his shoulder when my head made contact. "Easy, lass," he murmured as his finger penetrated my depths.

"Kalen," I panted out in a strangled whisper.

His finger thrust in and out of me several times before he pulled it out and released my dress. The stiff material didn't succumb to gravity as easily as, say, silk. He crossed his arm over my body, sucking his finger into his mouth. I glanced over my shoulder in time to catch it going in and I was just about undone. "You still taste as good as you look, delicious." He straightened and stepped back from me. "Too bad you didn't show up on time."

I was about to complain and say something vulgar when a couple saddled up to us and the red blob. "Interesting painting, isn't it?"

My face flushed, probably as red as the blob. "Yes, it is," I answered automatically.

I couldn't help but question if they'd seen what Kalen did. I refused to look at them and find out. When they stepped away, I turned, prepared to confront Kalen and maybe have a good laugh over our exploits, but he was gone.

Desperately, I strode down the main hall, searching for the man in each packed corridor. I was determined he wouldn't leave me like that.

"Bails, there you are," Lizzy said, stopping me.

When I saw her expression, I remembered who I was there for. I could find Kalen later as he most definitely wasn't off the hook. Still, this was her night.

"How's it going?" I asked. I'd tell her later about what had gone down. I didn't want to make this about me.

"It's great." She listed a string of A-list and up-and-coming actors. "They were all here, or so my assistant tells me." I wasn't surprised. "Not to mention I heard the names of a legendary rock star, the number one tennis player in the world, and Jeremy King." Looking perplexed, she said, "Apparently, they showed up and I didn't see any of them." She laughed, while I was stuck on the King name.

"Jeremy King? Is that the Money Man's name? I thought no one knew what he looked like?"

Her eyes popped. "Holy shit, Bails. I didn't think of that with everything else."

"Did you see him?"

She shook her head. "Maybe my assistant got it wrong?"

I thought of Anna.

"A colleague of mine said she saw him at work." I gave her the description Anna had given me.

"That's half the guys here, including Haven's beau."

A glance around the crowd confirmed that.

"Yeah, I guess," I said.

I didn't understand why I was so disappointed. It wasn't like I could date him even if I didn't have my hands full with Kalen. Dating a client was strictly prohibited. But the intrigue got me. The elusive, gorgeous male no one could pin down piqued my curiosity.

Lizzy's parents' words from that long-ago dinner played in my head. They'd suggested that the King's son, aka Money Man, might be playing games with the company's money. I had evidence that such a thing was true. Maybe if I saw him, I could get a read off him.

Not wanting to bring that up with Lizzy on her night, I pushed forward.

"It doesn't matter. This is an amazing event. I'm so happy for you," I said.

She didn't have to know that I'd been happily molested by Kalen in front of the blob.

"I'm selling out of stuff," she gushed. "I can't wait for drinks later. I need to celebrate. I'll just be a few more minutes. I'm trying to catch up with the countess."

She dashed off to meet with one of New York's socialites. I continued to walk the place and circled it again, wondering if I'd missed Kalen leaving while I was talking to Lizzy.

When my phone chirped, I nearly broke the fastening on my clutch to get it. It was well before nine. Where had Kalen gone?

"Hello," I said, sounding breathless as I made my way into a little alcove.

When he didn't speak, I thought for a second it might be another crank call until I finally heard his voice.

"Looking for me?" he teased, his voice rich and deep like chocolate.

"That's not fair," I said.

"You know what they say about payback." When I

rolled my eyes, he said, "Don't roll your eyes. I always finish what I start."

He'd stoked a fire when he'd touched me, and hearing his voice wasn't extinguishing the flames. I looked around but couldn't find him.

"Then why did you leave?" I asked.

"I had somewhere to be."

"Another meeting?"

He hesitated before saying, "No."

I closed my eyes and controlled my breathing. Calmly, I said, "I probably should have asked this earlier, but are you married?"

Who was I fooling? If he was, what were the odds he would be honest about it?

There was a longer pause before he spoke curtly, all teasing gone. "I said you were the only woman I'd be fucking, and I meant it."

His voice was a little on edge, but I didn't back down.

"You didn't answer my question."

"No, I'm not married or engaged or have a girlfriend," he snapped. "I have to go. I'll see you tomorrow at six as promised."

"Kalen," I said, hating where the conversation was going.

"Miss Glicks, I always keep my word," he said before disconnecting the call.

Tomorrow I would see him. But would it be the last time?

TWENTY-FOUR

I'D JUST SLIPPED MY PHONE INTO MY CLUTCH AND stepped back into the throng of people when Lizzy tugged my arm. "Hey, are you ready to blow this joint?"

I mustered up a smile. "Yes."

"Okay, give me a minute to close out the show."

I watched her stride right into the middle of the guests in the main gallery area, where she snagged a glass of wine from one of the waiters dressed in a traditional black and white uniform.

Spotting a waiter near me, I scooped up a glass myself.

Had I ruined things with Kalen because of my own insecurities? Then again, what was I ruining? He wasn't my boyfriend; he'd made that clear. Maybe it was better this way. Let him go before my heart could fall any deeper would be the smart thing to do.

Lizzy wasn't shy and had no problem speaking in front of large crowds. She showed her poise by thanking the guests for coming and for their patronage. Of course, she didn't say it like that. But after the toast, I took a long drink of the wine, feeling like life was far more complicated than I'd imagined growing up.

Once that was over, we escaped into Lizzy's cramped office, which was big enough for a desk and two chairs—one for her and one for a guest. She wasn't the type of person who needed a large space to validate who she was.

As we changed in her tiny space, it felt like old times, back in college, with us giggling at the prospect of going out. We weren't going to a club. We were headed to Lizzy's favorite dive bar and hangout.

Although it wasn't located too far from her place, it wasn't a pretentious yuppie bar. It was a little hole-in-the-wall that had stood the test of time. People who frequented the place weren't usually residents of the area, but rather those who worked nearby.

Not wanting to stand out amongst that crowd, we'd brought a change of clothes with us. Lizzy, a force to be reckoned with, wore tight jeans with knee-length boots over top. To complete the look, she wore a scoop neck "look at my cleavage" sweater, perfect for the chilly weather. She left her blonde hair in the cascading waves she'd worn for the showing.

If I didn't love Lizzy, I would be intimated in my jeans, ankle boots, and a turtleneck sweater in emerald green that made me think of Kalen's stunning eyes. A reminder I didn't need, considering how our conversation had ended.

When we walked into the bar, it was like being transported into another world. The crowd was most certainly not any Wilshire from Park Avenue.

We made our way to the bar, which was ahead on the right, running the length of the wall. Near the front were a few pool tables in use by a rowdy group of guys. Tables filled the middle, and beyond that was the tiny dance floor and a smattering of tables and chairs outlining the place. It was a Friday night, but the place wasn't that crowded, unlike the clubs in the area.

We found an opening and ordered drinks from a woman behind the bar.

"The usual, Piper," Lizzy said.

Piper nodded as her hard eyes kept a keen eye on everything that was going on. The bartender didn't look like she belonged, with a pretty face that could grace the cover of magazines. But it was her eyes that told another story.

Two drinks appeared in front of us. I sipped mine while Lizzy left me in favor of the dance floor as a popular song piped through the speakers.

I might have joined her if not for the melancholy I felt. Too bad I'd become invested in a man who wasn't invested in me. Lizzy waved me over, but I shook my head. As it turned out, she didn't need me. Guys had already begun to flock around her, caught by her infectious beauty and personality.

Eventually, she took a break and joined me. I eyed the door, longing for home, but I wouldn't tell her to stop. We hadn't hung out in a while.

Lizzy was facing the other end of the bar when a man who checked off every box on her fantasy man list walked in. My eyes must have widened, because she turned her head as he took off his worn leather jacket. When he hung it on the coat rack up front, we got a solid view of the black tee he wore. With his back to us, muscled arms revealed more art than Lizzy's gallery. My bestie turned back to me and mouthed, *holy shit*, right before he looked our way. He made his way around the bar to stand next to Lizzy as he hailed Piper. I glanced at the well-worn black jeans and boots he wore.

Clearly lust at first sight, Lizzy gave me a look that asked for my opinion. I nodded imperceptibly just before Piper came over and Lizzy's fantasy spoke.

"Beer," was all he said. His voice was gruff and deep. I thought Lizzy would melt right there on the barstool. Smoothly, she turned to him. He gave us a quick look and said, "Ladies," before taking his beer and heading over to the pool tables.

Another bartender who happened to walk over at the same time laughed. He was Lizzy's type too. But his long-time girlfriend, who was just as heavily tattooed as he was, was working the tables. She stood nearly as tall as her man and taller than Lizzy, and looked like she could kick both of our asses at the same time. So we didn't flirt with him. "I see you girls like him."

"You know him?" Lizzy asked with no shame.

"Not really. He's only been in a few times," he answered.

"Do you know his name?" Lizzy pressed.

"I've heard some of the guys call him Striker, but I'm not sure if they were just referring to his pool skills." Before she could ask anything else, he was called over to fill more orders.

After he walked away, I asked, "What about Hans?"

She smiled. "What about him? We aren't married or exclusive. Besides, there's no harm in flirting."

Once Lizzy decided on a guy, he was sure to be hers

before the night was over. I pitied him as she tossed her hair over one shoulder with determination in her face. The guy stood no chance at all.

It didn't take long for a different guy to come over and ask her to dance. She accepted, clearly using it as a way to pull Striker's attention her way. Glances between the two of them told me that he had, in fact, noticed her with someone else. But he made no move toward her. Instead, he seemed serious about his pool game. Once I saw money exchanging hands, I knew that he was all business.

Lizzy must have noticed too. A few games later, when no one took him on, she stopped dancing and sashayed over to him. With the music and other noise of the bar, I couldn't hear what they said before she took a cue stick from the available ones on the wall.

Trying not to all-out stare, I watched in horror when his head did a quick shake no and he strode off toward the door. Slipping on his jacket, he headed outside, leaving my best friend stunned. The narrowing of her eyes indicated how pissed she was.

Once she caught my gaze, she straightened her features and headed over. "You ready to blow?" she asked.

Hell, I'd been ready to leave long ago. Because she didn't bring him up, I didn't either. "Yeah," I said.

After paying the tab, we headed out and there he was, on a tricked-out Harley, smoking a cigarette. Lizzy, unperturbed, strode to the street to hail a cab, which was unlike her as she used Uber on the regular. I followed as she ignored Striker and the other man he was speaking to, though I knew better. The guy standing with Striker did take notice and approached us.

"I can give you a ride," the guy said to Lizzy with a broad smirk, eyeing her up and down.

"Don't bother with the princess," Striker said.

"Why not?" the guy said. "I'd bend a knee to get some of that."

Lizzy gave the guy a coy smile. Striker revved his engine to life and said in words that could be heard over the noise, "A girl like her only wants to brag to her friends about slumming." And he peeled off.

"Bastard," Lizzy called after him, losing her cool.

"Hey, I don't mind if you slum with me," the guy said.

Rolling her eyes, she raised her hand and hailed the passing cab, which came to a stop next to us. I slid into the back seat next to her, speechless, unable to comprehend what had just happened. Never had I seen a guy so blatantly turn her down. I was at a loss as to what I should or should not say to my best friend. What had just happened was so unprecedented. The way Striker had so summarily shut her down made me think about the ever-elusive Kalen and what he was doing at that very moment.

TWENTY-FIVE

THE CAB RIDE HOME WAS QUIET. IT WAS LATE, WELL past midnight, and Lizzy headed straight for her room despite my words of encouragement: *He's an asshole. You deserve better.*

Alone in my room, the cold sheets kept me awake. I wanted Kalen instead of empty space.

My fitful sleep was filled with dreams of him. In them, I stood on the lush green plains of the Highlands as my kilted Scotsman rode off into battle, no doubt conjured up by the historical romance novel I'd been reading. It only left me wanting more of him.

Morning wasn't much better. Lizzy was gone. She'd left a note that Hans was taking her to a photo shoot and after they planned to head off somewhere for a picnic.

Again, I was envious of the easy way she bounced back from the night before.

To keep my mind busy, I decided to work from home. I wrote up my findings with the list of transactions and the staging number they totaled. I hadn't decided if I should just send it to Scott or include the partner-in-charge on the email. Scott would consider it a betrayal if I did. But this was way bigger than both of us, if I was right. If I was wrong, it could spell the end of my career. The best option was to talk it through with Scott on Monday, then decide.

I hand wrote a letter to my mother I would mail. It had been a while and I missed her and my siblings. Not wanting to live in the community permanently didn't mean I didn't miss it. My life there hadn't been bad.

By five, my stomach was all aflutter. Up until that point, I hadn't been sure what to wear. I stood in the mirror, having showered and put on makeup, which for me probably took longer than it did for most since I didn't wear it every day.

I held up two dresses, one black and one nearly white. Both from Lizzy. She'd left a few choices hanging on my door. I chose the strapless black with the slit to the thigh. With Lizzy being so tall, I had to pair it with stiletto heels so the hem didn't drag on the floor.

A call from the downstairs didn't precede the knock on my door. Yet I wasn't surprised to see Kalen on the other side. I opened the door to find him wearing a crisp white shirt, bowtie, and dark jacket and pants. He looked classically handsome with his dark hair neatly tousled on his head.

"Tha thu bòidheach."

I had no idea what that meant. If not for his heated gaze on me, I would have taken it as a curse, especially the way he muttered it under his breath.

"You know, I can go by myself because I'm not going to apologize for pissing you off because I asked if you were married. Though I admit my timing was off and I should have asked sooner."

We traded glares until he finally broke the silence.

"As I've said, I'm a man of my word."

"Well, I'm freeing you of your obligation. You don't exactly seem happy about being here."

Neither one of us had moved, as if the door's threshold was the proverbial line in the sand.

"If I dinnae want to be here, I wouldn't be, Miss Glicks."

Grrr. We were back to Miss Glicks. If my emotions weren't on some roller coaster I couldn't get off of, I might have been smug that I picked up on one of Kalen's tells. When he was angry, or passionate for that matter, his native tongue broke into his perfect English.

"What if I don't want you here?" I snapped.

His eyes drifted down my body like a caress. When our eyes connected again, he said, "Your nipples are like diamond shards poking through your dress. I dinnae have to touch you to know you're wet. You want me to fuck you, but I won't."

Sounding as silly as I felt, I said, "Fuck you," and stepped the few feet to Lizzy's favorite chair to grab my coat and clutch.

Then I brushed by him, closing the door in the process.

"Fine, if we're going to go, we should leave now. The sooner we get there, the sooner this night is over."

I couldn't stomp in the high heels without potentially

tripping myself. But I did my best damn impression. I stabbed at the elevator like my life depended on it, but it refused to light.

Kalen's heat warmed my back, though he didn't touch me until his hand caught my wrist. Gently, he removed it after my unsuccessful attempts to call the elevator. He let go and smoothly tapped the button that lit up as if it had been waiting for a kinder touch.

I counted off sixty seconds, trying to rein in everything I was feeling. He'd been right. Though I'd felt righteous indignation, I was also more turned on than I had been since we'd met.

When the doors finally parted, we stepped in and stood in opposite corners like fighters before a match.

That was when my composure slipped. I let my wandering eyes fall to just below Kalen's belt.

The smirk that played over my mouth was like victory. "It seems like I'm not the only one who wants to fuck," I said, staring pointedly at the swell of his cock and the imprint it made in his pants.

"I never said I didn't want to fuck you, Miss Glicks," he said coolly. "I only said I wouldn't."

I almost dared him to before I was saved by the bell. The doors opened and a clingy couple stepped in effectively between us. The woman held onto her boyfriend's arm and stared adoringly up at him, or so it looked in the reflective surface facing them. I rolled my eyes and kept them off of Kalen. It was going to be a long night.

We followed the touchy-feely couple into the night. At the curb sat the most stunning car I had ever seen and I'm not much of a car girl, growing up without the luxury.

It was a Mercedes. I knew that much from the medallion on the hood. Scott owned one, but it looked like a junker compared to this.

A vision in midnight blue with an extremely long hood, low roofline, and short rear was something to look at. The multi-spoked wheels mirrored the grill and took my breath away.

I hadn't realized I'd stopped until Kalen's hand landed on my back.

"Come," he said.

I looked up at him and caught his smug grin. I wanted to growl in frustration. My being mesmerized by his car felt like a win in his column.

Lizzy would have loved the inside of the car with its stark white interior, which just fit.

It purred to life as I took in all that I could see, including the bright blue panoramic touch screen.

"Do you like it?" he asked.

It was an understatement. And though I still wasn't happy with him, I wouldn't lie.

"Yes, it's unlike anything I've ever seen."

"It's a Maybach 6 Cabriolet. A Vision Mercedes concept car, practically one of a kind," he said, almost wistfully.

All of that went over my head except that it was rare. "How did you get one?"

The hint of a smile died from his lips and flatlined.

"Part of my employment agreement."

"Your skills must be in high demand," I said, not thinking about the double entendre when the words escaped my mouth.

"Not really. My father wants me at his company. I made it a condition in my contract, thinking there would be no way he could fulfill it."

I was surprised by his candor, but didn't let that stop me from asking more.

"You didn't want to work for him?"

He thought about it a second. "I wanted him to fail and be forced to beg me to work for him."

His frankness relaxed some of my earlier tension as he opened up to me.

"He wasn't a good dad?" I asked.

"More like an absent one. When my parents split, we had no contact until he needed me."

Though I wanted to know more, I decided not to press my luck. I went for a softer question.

"Do you have any siblings?"

"A half-brother he fathered while married to my mother. And who knows, there might be more out there. I'm sure his funeral will be full of them."

A bitter bite chilled his words, so I extended an olive branch. He'd shared some of himself, and I would do the same.

"I have seven brothers and sisters," I said and watched as his brows lifted. "I have an older sister and my youngest sister is four." I thought about how I had only seen her once and nearly choked up. "It makes me sad I won't get to see her grow up."

A pinprick of tears stung the back of my eyes.

"You can't go visit?" he asked.

"It's complicated." I took a deep breath. "Have you ever heard of a simple lifestyle?"

"Living without excess," he guessed.

That was close.

"Sort of. Are you familiar with Amish people?"

He nodded. My eyes strayed to my ring. I had almost forgotten about it, which surprised me. Movement forced my eyes back to the enigmatic man I was with.

"Well, it's like that but not. We live without much interference with technology. However, we do have a minimal amount. Like our community has a phone and a computer. It's locked away and used only when absolutely needed. Anyway, to put it mildly, by going to college as a woman and on top of that not going back to use my skills for our community basically makes me an outcast. I'm too worldly and may corrupt the young minds of my siblings, not to mention other children there."

I fell silent after releasing the tight band of knots I'd held so close for years.

"You can never go back?"

That wasn't the right question.

"I can go. But there are lots of rules, and it's always hard to come from the world of jeans and yoga pants and back to only wearing modest skirts and dresses."

I caught his slight wince. Now he understood what his command about wearing dresses had felt like for me.

"That's where your defiance about me asking you to wear skirts comes from?"

A glance down at my dress was a reminder I didn't hate them. "It's not that I mind. Dresses are perfect for certain occasions and I own some cute skirts. It's the demand to wear one that takes me back to the few choices I had growing up."

We fell silent but not for long.

"We're here," he said.

I looked up and saw The Metropolitan Museum on our right.

"I've never been here before," I said absently.

It felt like I was in some sort of dream. There I was at The Met, with the most handsome man I'd ever laid eyes on in an eye-turning car.

"At midnight, will I turn into a pumpkin?" I muttered.

"What?"

His question shook me out of my daydream. I hadn't realized I'd spoken out loud until that moment.

"Nothing," I said.

We were in a line of cars waiting for a valet.

"Your firm must have some pull. They don't normally host corporate events on a Saturday."

That gave me pause. "How would you know that?"

He didn't seem like an event planner.

His broad shoulders lifted in a half-shrug. "It came up in a meeting when we were planning our holiday party."

"I wasn't in on the planning, but I know it's a party not only for employees, but our clients as well," I said.

A man came over and opened my car door. I got out and did a little three-sixty, soaking everything in. When I stopped, I caught sight of Kalen handing the valet a fifty.

Kalen was rich. On some level I knew. But the car, his tip, and the tux that fit him perfectly all spoke of money— lots of it. I felt a little uncomfortable. As much as I wanted away from my life back home, I didn't fit well in Lizzy's world, and Kalen's was starting to appear a whole lot bigger.

"Shall we?"

I glanced up into those glorious green eyes and took the arm he offered. He escorted me inside the museum like a prince holding his princess.

My glass slippers shattered when we walked into the great hall and smack into my nemesis.

TWENTY-SIX

TOO STUNNED TO MOVE, IT TOOK KALEN'S GUIDING hand to get me moving forward. It wasn't exactly Scott who had taken me by surprise. It was the evidence of his betrayal tucked at his side, glowing as they say. Thankfully, Scott was too self-involved to notice me. His conversation with some of the firm's partners even took precedence over the woman next to him.

"Let me take your coat, lass."

That caught my attention. I was lass again and wasn't sure how to take it.

I shrugged out of it and watched Kalen walk it over to the coat check before I moved into an alcove and placed a call.

The phone rang on the other end a few times before a breathy "Hello" answered.

"I'm sorry, Lizzy. Is it a bad time?"

Muffled noise grew quieter before I heard a door close.

"No, what's up? Are you with that delicious man of yours?"

Kalen wasn't mine. That much I was sure of.

"I don't know. I think this is a mistake."

I imagined Lizzy's grim face as she spoke. "Don't tell me Scott is getting to you?"

"It's not that," I hurried to say, but she cut me off before I could explain.

"Is it your conscience? I swear, Bails, I don't understand what your parents did to you. They are a product of the seventies. You'd think they know better."

I didn't quite understand her context.

"What do you mean by the seventies?"

"You really need a lesson in pop culture. The seventies birthed sexual freedom and no judgment from choice. You need to own yours." She sighed. "Screw the hell out of the edible man of yours or not without shame."

"He's not my man," I said.

"He could be."

"No, he was very clear about that."

"And you, my friend, have a lot to learn. That man is hooked. All you have to do is reel him in."

A man's voice called for Lizzy.

"I have to go," she said, sounding resigned.

"I'm sorry. I should have asked how things were going with you. I hope I didn't interrupt."

She laughed. "No, you interrupted nothing but a room full of pretentious people. Tell me again why I'm dating a man who runs in the same circles I do?"

I wasn't going to remind her she was doing it for her parents. Instead, I turned her advice to me back on her.

"Your choice. You don't have to do anything you don't want."

"Touché, my friend. Touché. See you at home later."

"Yeah."

We ended the call and I tucked my phone back into my clutch. I walked out into the open and found Kalen surveying the landscape of people.

"Looking for me?" I asked a moment later as I stepped in front of him.

"Dannan, an còmhnaidh,"

I would have asked what he meant if not for my name spoken by the devil himself.

"Bailey."

Slowly, I spun around to face the enemy. I kept my eyes level on him, not feeling anything, not even anger.

"I'm surprised to see you here," Scott said.

"And why is that?" I asked, my snarkiness not going unnoticed.

He wasn't given the chance to answer as Kalen stepped up beside me. He slid his arm around my waist and a shiver ran through me. I had to swallow, creating an awkward second to pass as Scott noticed Kalen's possessive hold on me.

"Lass, aren't you going to introduce me?"

Scott's eyesore began to fan herself, trying to draw attention her way.

She muttered, "Lass. I wish you would call me lass, Scott."

I ignored her to dispense with the unpleasantries. Scott didn't even glance in her direction, his eyes bouncing between my date and me.

"Kalen, this is Scott Hayes. Scott, this is—"

"Kalen Brinner," Kalen said, extending a hand.

It was comical the way Scott mooned over Kalen's wrist like he'd seen the Holy Grail.

"Is that a limited edition 5531 Patek Philippe?"

I caught a hint of golden metal before Kalen snatched his arm away from Scott, who didn't appear to want to let go. As Kalen straightened his cuffs, Scott babbled like a man in love.

"I myself have an eye on a 5522 Calatrava Pilot, which is a dream. Although I expect my bonus to be enough to cover it."

Scott's mistress, tired of being ignored, lifted her arm and waved it between us.

"I guess smart watches are obsolete."

But it wasn't the watch she wanted attention on. It was my former engagement ring that graced her finger. I didn't give her the satisfaction of focusing on it. Instead, I kept my eyes on hers.

"Kalen, this is Melba," I said so saccharine sweetly, I almost had to lick my lips.

"Melissa," she corrected.

I wasn't really mad at Scott anymore. The spineless little weasel's cheating was most likely enviable. He was just that kind of guy. This woman, however, had relentlessly pursued him while smiling in my face. If I hadn't known her, I wouldn't have been angry with her. And even though we'd never been friends, the knife in my back didn't hurt any less.

Kalen didn't take her offered hand and I wanted to laugh at her disappointment.

"I would say it was nice seeing you again, Scott. But that would be a lie, and that's your specialty."

"For your information, I didn't send you any letter," Scott's fiancée said as I walked away.

I hesitated for a second but didn't turn around. It took me a moment to remember the warning letter I'd given Scott and told him to have his fiancée back off. But would she really be honest about not sending it? Of course not. I shook off the bad vibe I got and waltzed away from the man I once thought I loved. Truth was, I'd loved the idea we created. I'd never loved him. Not completely, anyway.

We wound our way through the crowd, Kalen following my lead. I aimed toward the center buffet with a spread of canapés and hors d'oeuvres. However, it was the waiter with the tray of wine glasses that caught my eye. I relieved him of one before he disappeared to my disappointment. I had a feeling I would need several more to get through the night.

"Was he your former fiancé?" Kalen asked as I drained my drink.

I nodded and swept my eyes, looking for another waiter nearby.

"He's a skeekit tadger."

I giggled. The wine might have gone to my head. "I like the sound of that. Before I can use it, I need to know what it means."

"I think you can guess," he teased. His eyes lifted over my shoulder and narrowed. "Give me a minute."

He stalked off and I turned around, wondering who he was going to talk to. Though I was blatantly aware he wasn't taking me. Then again, how would one introduce one's fuck buddy?

I closed my eyes, wondering again what I was doing.

When I opened them again, I'd been cornered by Scott's parents. *Great*.

"Bailey Glicks," his father said, superiority written all over his face.

Good manners forced a placid smile on my face.

"It's good to see you, Mr. and Mrs. Hayes."

I traded handshakes with his father, and then half-hugs and air kisses with his mother.

"Scott tells me you've found a way to work together," Mr. Hayes said.

It was the reminder that his father was a partner in the firm, and I had to play nice.

"We have," I admitted.

"That's good, especially since Scott has found some interesting transactions that need further investigation."

"You mean, I found. Scott assigned me—"

He waved me off. "I'm sure you're going to continue to work under my son and perform your duties. If you'll excuse me."

I ground my teeth as he left me alone with his wife. First thing Monday, I would send the email I'd composed earlier following up on my findings and would cc the partner-in-charge. While I respected the chain of command, there was no way Scott would screw me over at work too.

"I'm disappointed in you, Bailey."

I gawked at Scott's mother. "What?"

She tsked me. "You must have learned by now this is a man's world."

The woman before me no longer seemed like the woman I'd admired. She had poise and beauty I'd respected until now. "But we women have our own kind of power and you let my son get away," she said.

Respectful, yes. A pacifist I was not.

"Your son was cheating on me," I said, certain I wasn't hearing her correctly. "There is no denying that."

Her humorless laugh barely curled her lips. "Yes, well, that was a mistake that could have been hidden away if you stayed. Instead, she wears your ring and that baby in her belly like an award."

Scott's soon-to-be-wife was very pregnant, something I noticed when I first walked into the party, causing my steps to falter. It had been another blow to have confirmation that his cheating hadn't been a one-time thing like he'd claimed. But I wouldn't let Scott derail my life anymore.

"Don't be a child, Bailey. Men cheat. But they usually don't marry their whores."

I couldn't help the belly laugh I barked out. "Maybe that's okay in your world, but not in mine."

In retrospect, that was the moment I should have walked away.

"And what, you think the man you came with in the five-thousand-dollar suit, wearing a half-million-dollar watch, will settle for just you, a small-town girl with no family connections? Haven't you noticed all the women checking him out? He could have any one of them with the snap of his finger. Including you. But most of the women here would understand and accept the world he lives in. If you can't handle Scott, my dear, you most definitely cannot handle that man."

I had no snappy comebacks. She'd played on my insecurities like a seasoned pro. As she disappeared from my line of sight, I spotted Kalen talking to a well-dressed older man. It shouldn't have bothered me that he didn't see me worthy of meeting this person he knew.

The gallery looked inviting and I took the stairs up to get some space.

Above the main room, I easily found Kalen now talked to a tall and gorgeous brunette. The inviting look she gave him was everything Scott's mother spoke of. Why was I deluding myself? She was exactly right. This wasn't my world.

When I looked again, Kalen was gone. I swept my eyes over the crowd, knowing it would be easy to find Kalen's tall and broad features, but I felt him instead.

His big hands gripped my waist as his breath fanned over my neck.

"This is where you've been hiding."

I wanted to say I hadn't been hiding. But heat licked over my skin like a brushfire. My body was a raging inferno by the time I turned in his arms. It would have been easy to give in as Kalen's penetrating eyes shadowed in inky black were focused on me.

"We can't do this," I protested, seeing nothing but five-alarm desire in his gaze.

"Do what?" he asked, like he wasn't at all affected. "Fuck?"

I stepped back, only to be cut short by the railing. I twisted a bit to lean against a column.

"Any of it," I said, more sternly than I felt.

"Are you backing out of our agreement? Because we both know you secretly want my cock buried deep inside you, right here, right now."

God, the man was sin incarnate.

"As much as I want to, I can't do this casual thing. I wasn't built to be unaffected."

He studied me. "You're saying you want a commitment."

I wasn't sure what I wanted, just what I didn't want.

"I'm saying I don't want to be a dirty little secret."

He closed the distance, leaving me nowhere to go.

"You aren't a dirty little secret," he said, his menacing eyes held on mine.

I stiffened my spine and stood a little straighter. "Really? You couldn't seem to get away fast enough to talk to someone you knew without bothering to introduce me. Which is stupid on my part because we aren't in a relationship. This is why I can't do this."

His kissable lips lifted in a knowing smile. "You're jealous."

"Yes. Which is also stupid. We've never had sex in a bed, not really if you exclude using the edge of it like a prop. I don't even know where you live. You've never invited me to your place. Thus, leaving questions in my mind like if you're married. And you owe me nothing."

I didn't wait to see victory on his face. I'd already lost too much tonight and now sounded like a hysterical woman. I slipped around the column.

"I'm ready to go home. I can catch a cab," I said.

I didn't look back as I dashed away as fast as my heels would allow. I assumed Kalen hadn't followed until I got to the front. I turned, remembering I couldn't get my coat without him.

He was there pocketing his phone. He stepped forward and produced the marker needed to get our garments.

"I brought you here. I'll take you home," he said quietly but determined.

There was no way for me to be impervious. Every word out of the man's mouth was like a stroke over my clit. Then there was his touch as he innocently helped me into my coat.

He led me to his amazing car as if he'd contacted the valet before we exited the building, and maybe he had. I should have stayed at least until I'd spoken to the partner-in-charge of my current assignment. But it was too late.

I closed my eyes on the drive home. I couldn't look at the man and not remember riding his cock in a different car not so long ago.

When the car engine died, I thought maybe I'd fallen asleep. The ride seemed way too short for me to be home and too eerily quiet.

I opened my eyes and blinked a few times. We were in an underground garage where a dozen or more spectacular cars were parked.

"Where are we?" I asked, amazed and a little shocked as I guessed the answer.

"You wanted to know where I lived." My mouth fell open. He, on the other hand, didn't lack for words. "You can go upstairs with me or I can take you home."

The smart answer would have been home. Curiosity about the man won out as Lizzy's suggestion played in my head. Did I have more power in this chess match between us than I thought? My queen to his king?

"What does this mean?" I asked, not moving yet.

"It means you're the first woman I've brought home."

"Ever?" I asked, feeling more like a pawn to his knight.

"Yes," he said, his focus sharp on me. "Except those in my employ."

"Why now?" That was a dumb question. Hadn't I made that somewhat of an ultimatum, though I hadn't meant to?

"Because I'm not ready to let you go."

He got out of the car, had my door open, and his hand held out for mine before I could completely process what was happening.

"Are you coming?" he asked.

I was in a fog, but my body wasn't. I took his proffered hand and got out. It felt even more surreal when we entered the elevator.

He produced a black card he held against a reader. A digital keypad appeared, and he keyed in a code before he pressed his thumb to a square. A voice too serene to be human asked for his name.

"Brinner," he said, with that amazing accent of his.

"Voice authenticated," it said, and the elevator began to move without him entering a floor.

"That's pretty high-tech," I said.

He pivoted to face me. "Four layers of security, not easy to crack."

"Why not? If someone had your card, code, and a copy of your fingerprint," I began.

"The scanner has a heat signature. There must be blood flowing through my veins for that to work. Enough about that. That dress has had me hard all night."

His hand found the slit as he palmed my thigh. His thumb snapped at the garters I'd worn just for him.

"Fuck, lass. I said I wasn't going to fuck you, but I lied. I'm going to own your pussy until you beg me to stop."

He circled a finger around my nub until I was whimpering. Then the elevator stopped. The doors parted into a lavish and spacious apartment. I caught a flash of minimal furniture set on dark wooden floors that led to a panel of windows that lined the wall. Through them a lit-up New York cityscape could be seen. A floating, twisting staircase set to the side led upstairs to places unknown.

I took off in that direction, knowing I wanted to be caught. I crashed into the wall as his big body covered mine.

"You want to play," he said, voice so deep it came out as a growl.

I wanted his lips on mine, but instead, he teased my ear and down my neck. Then my dress was shoved down so his mouth could consume my breast. With every lick and suck, I squeezed my legs tight, afraid I'd come just that easily. As I climbed toward ecstasy, he knelt. He busied his hands by parting my dress at the slit and shoving aside the scrap of fabric that covered my mound. Then he licked a path from my clit to my opening and back again as I panted with need.

With the perfect amount of suction on my nub and the addition of two perfectly curled and pumping fingers, I came apart, coating him with all my pleasure.

I didn't think I could stand. But he could. First my coat and then his hit the floor. His nimble fingers worked at freeing me of my dress. It pooled at my feet as he lifted me off mine. I wound my legs around his and buried my face in his neck, afraid my liquid muscles couldn't hang on.

"It should be my turn," I whispered.

"We have all night for that," he promised. "First, I'm going to have you in my bed."

His bed. Was this real? My eyes were so heavy, I could hardly keep them open as he took me upstairs. All the sleepless nights were catching up to me. And for the first time in years, I felt safe with a man.

He crawled onto the mattress and laid me on the bed underneath him as he hovered above.

"You're a vision, lass, like you've always belonged here."

He sat back and undid the bowtie at his neck before he began the task of unbuttoning his shirt. When I reached to help, he caught my hand. "Just lie there and let me look at you."

His request made me want to squirm, self-consciousness easing in like an old friend.

"Part your legs, lass, and remind me how sweet you taste."

He wedged himself between my thighs as I slowly complied to his request. He snapped the string to my thong, and I opened myself to him, leaving my pussy more exposed.

In one unguarded moment, I gave in to my wants and stroked a hand down my abdomen. I grazed my fingertips over my overly sensitive parts, throwing my head back on a moan.

I lifted up, needing more than ever to touch the bulge in his pants. He shrugged off his shirt and tossed it onto the floor somewhere. As I went to stroke him through his pants, he captured my wrist and pinned me to the bed with my hands over my head.

"Not yet."

His throaty words had me writhing underneath him.

"Please," I begged. "I need to touch you."

He shook his head. "I want you to watch as I sink my cock into that pretty cunt of yours." He reached for something on the bed. "Now, are you going to be a good girl and keep your hands here?"

He tapped where they lay above my head and I nodded.

"Good girl."

Back on his knees, he unzipped his pants at an unholy slow pace. I was greedy and almost moved to helped but managed to stay still just as his dick sprang free.

Once that deed was done, he picked up speed, shedding his pants in no time.

He gripped that big dick of his in one hand and rubbed the plum head through my wet folds.

"Watch your pussy swallow my cock."

I lifted on my arms to see him inch his thick shaft slowly into my pussy. Spread wide, my inner walls accommodated his girth. As pain mixed with pleasure, I fell to my back and panted. He worked magic, fingering my clit and lifting my hip with his other hand. At the new angle, pleasure won over pain.

When he achingly bottomed out at my womb, he bent to suck one of my nipples as he slowly pulled out. Wanting more, I clamped my legs around his waist and arched my hips so he would hit bottom again.

"Greedy little wench, aren't you?"

"More," I cried, doing my best to impale myself on him.

"And so you shall have."

In the blink of an eye, he untwisted my legs, flipped me over, and had my ass high in the air before plunging back in.

I might have screamed a little as I orgasmed just that quick. I fisted the sheets as his tempo picked up, milking my climax for all it was worth.

He bent over and cupped my breast while leaving a trail of light kisses up my spine. When he got to my neck, he rolled us over to our sides, still deep inside me. His thrusts continued, though he lifted my top leg to curl over his as he plunged deeper.

I was spiraling fast to another orgasm as his fingers played my pussy like a song.

"Tha thu a 'mhèinn," he said lyrically before his cock jerked inside me, filling me with his hot seed as my inner walls spasmed around him.

I lay limp and limber while he stayed wrapped around me. My eyes were closed in a drowsy slumber when I asked, "What did you say?"

"Tha thu a 'mhèinn," he repeated. When I nodded, he said, "Roughly translated, you're mine."

"Is that what I am?" I asked, feeling like I was wrapped in sunshine.

"I don't think I have a choice," he said as if he could hardly believe it himself.

I rolled away from him so fast, his softening cock was ripped free from my pussy.

"I'm not forcing you to do anything," I complained, feeling stupid again.

His smile only irritated me more.

"I love that fire in your eyes, lass." I narrowed them in response. "What I meant is, I can't let you go. I want to get to know you better and see where this goes, though my life is complicated."

It wasn't a promise and I pressed my lips together, wanting to believe and trust him.

"Okay," I said, softening. "You first. Tell me where you're from."

Though I knew he was from Scotland, I wanted to know more.

"My father met my mother in Scotland. Married her and brought her here where I was born. For a time, I think she was happy. But soon, neglect and his cheating caused her to go back home with me."

Though I'd heard some of the story, this was a little more of the puzzle.

"I'm sorry."

"It's not your fault. It's his. He never came looking for either of us. Since my mom's parents warned her not to marry *that American*, we were on our own."

Unable to imagine what it would be like to grow up wanting, I kept quiet.

"There were times when food was scarce, and clothes were well worn and too small. But we made do."

I was at a loss. We weren't rich back home, but no one went hungry. We made clothes and shared things that didn't fit anymore or sewed new ones.

"Don't cry for me," he said, stroking a finger over the moisture on my face.

I hadn't realized a tear spilled until that moment.

"I hate that for you," I said.

"It made me stronger." He held a hand out to the room. "These things don't mean anything to me. They are my father's penance as if he could make up for all his neglect."

I finally took a glance around at the tan textured walls

with gray washed furniture set on deep brown wooden floors. It was simple yet elegant. Something a man and even a woman could love.

But it was hearing that he wasn't materialistic that warmed my heart.

"What about you?" he asked.

"My community is located in a small town in Pennsylvania. I lived there all my life until I went to college in Boston. And now I'm here."

"You've never been anywhere else?"

I shook my head. "No, though I'd gotten my passport to travel for my honeymoon."

My mood soured some.

He tipped up my chin. "Don't worry, lass. You'll see the world."

It was the perfect moment for him to kiss me. When he didn't, I rolled off the bed to hide my disappointment.

"Can I use your bathroom?" I asked as he stared at me.

I resisted the urge to cover myself. No shame. He'd already seen all of me. I walked in my garter and heels to the place he pointed and shut myself inside as his cum began its slow descent from the force of gravity.

Why wouldn't he kiss me? It didn't make sense. I cupped my hand to my mouth to check my breath, but it wasn't me. I wanted to turn back around and ask him right away. But he'd given me so much in a short period of time, I could wait a little longer to probe him more.

Unsure of protocol, I turned on the shower to think it through while I cleaned up. Should I leave? The last time I dated a man was Scott. I'd been living in a college dorm, and that had set the rules on how long he could stay.

I sat on the edge of a large tub as I took off my heels and thigh-highs, removing my garter last. I stared in the large mirror before stepping into the large glass shower. Jets hit me at all angles, from the top and several in the front. I squirted shampoo from a bottle onto my hands and lathered my hair. That was when I heard the door open.

He said nothing, coming in and placing warm soapy hands on me. He worked at washing my body as I rinsed my hair. When his hands slipped between my legs, embers of desire were stoked into flames.

"I need to be inside you again."

He'd just lifted me off my feet when a female voice rang out, calling his name.

We both froze.

TWENTY-SEVEN

Slowly, he set me down, haunted eyes on mine. He didn't say a word. Just exited and wrapped a towel around his waist. I was left to wonder who it was.

If it was nobody, wouldn't he have said something?

Fresh tears sprang from my eyes as my head went for the worst possible options. I turned off the shower and grabbed another convenient towel to cover myself. *Two towels, Bailey. What do you think that means?*

I crept to the door and opened it a crack. Over the railing and down into the living room, my gaze found the intruders: a woman and someone else.

Kalen stood before them in jogging pants and a tee shirt wet from the shower. The woman didn't move as she listened to words I couldn't hear. But it was the sweet-faced boy with dark hair, a spitting image of his father, who caught my entire attention. Especially when Kalen scooped him up.

I lost my breath and moved back to the bathroom to gather my things. Then I searched for my purse. I didn't remember dropping it anywhere. I ended up finding it on the floor in the bedroom. Silently as I could, I took the steps two at a time. The living room was empty when I entered and I made a mad dash to the elevator, reaching for my dress and coat before jabbing at the call button.

It arrived silently just as I had my dress zipped halfway up. Kalen was nowhere to be found. I got in the elevator and found only one button and it was marked L. I was grateful for that and quickly pushed it, praying Kalen wouldn't emerge from a hidden doorway, catching me on the run. I worried with his security I would need him to leave. I pulled on my coat and ran a hand through my wet hair.

As expected, I ended up on the ground floor. The doorman was there opening the door on the frigid night. My damp hair would end up being the death of me if my mother were to be believed.

"Miss, do you need a cab?"

I nodded, not having the willpower to pull up my phone for other options. I took the chance of catching a cold, or worse pneumonia, and stepped out behind him. He blew a whistle and waved a hand, and one arrived within moments. I shivered as I rattled off my address and tried to regain my warmth. My head spun with what I'd seen.

How could I be so stupid? Did I have "gullible" written on my forehead? Was this punishment for leaving Turner? Karma was a bitch.

With unsteady fingers, I brought up Lizzy's phone number and dialed. It rang and rang with no answer. It wasn't terribly late. She was probably still out with Hans.

After I arrived and paid the cabbie, I turned off my

phone. Kalen hadn't called, and I wasn't sure why it bothered me more than anything else that had happened. I guess I'd hoped he would have had some excuse to explain the unexplainable.

When I reached my door, I found an envelope with my name scrawled across it taped to the door. I took it down after I unlocked the door. As soon as I got inside, I spotted an unopened bottle of wine on the counter. I tossed the envelope next to it, shrugged out of my coat, and tossed it over the sofa. Then I bypassed the wine and opted for a pint of Magnum's Double Sea Salt Caramel ice cream. The satisfying crunch as I cracked the top layer brought a faint smile to my face. Men sucked, but ice cream ruled.

I'd eaten half when I remembered the letter addressed to me. I went back for it. The paper stock was fancy, with gold foil on the inside. I pulled out the thick card stock and nearly dropped it when I read the message. *Last warning*.

Had I been wrong? Was it Kalen's wife and not Scott's mistress who was sending me the notes? It made a weird kind of sense, though I had no way of knowing how she found out so much about me. Then again, she was rich. And money could buy everything, or so the saying went.

Then I heard it and prayed the sound of thundering footsteps was Lizzy's. But I was fooling myself. The pounding steps were too heavy to be my best friend's.

"Bailey, let me in," preceded a fist beating on the door.

I got up, though I had no intention of doing what he asked.

"Please, leave," I said through the door as goosebumps popped up over my skin.

"Let me explain."

His sexy, deep brogue now only made me protectively wrap my arms around myself as if I could stop the sting of betrayal.

"Go back to your wife," *and son*, I inwardly added.

A son. I hadn't allowed myself to acknowledge that until now.

"She's not my wife."

"Fine, girlfriend. Whatever. It doesn't matter. Just leave."

I turned my back to the door and sagged a little. I felt foolish, naïve, everything Scott's mother had claimed me to be.

"She's not my girlfriend."

"Your son's mother."

There, I'd said it out loud. And idiotically, I hoped he'd dispute that claim too.

"She's my nanny."

That didn't make things better. He did have a son. And the headlines these days were riddled with married men cheating on their wives with their nannies.

"That doesn't mean you aren't sleeping with her."

"She's my cousin, lass. We're helping each other out."

"And where is your son's mother?"

I held in a breath.

"Out of the picture."

"Whatever. Just tell her to stop with the notes. We're done."

"Notes?" he asked.

"It doesn't matter," I said with as much resolve as I could muster. "You lied to me. I can't trust you."

The door rattled as his hand hit it. "Lass, I've never lied

to yer. I didn't tell you about my son because it's not something I bring up to strangers."

"Exactly. We're strangers. So, you can leave and forget all about me."

He growled in frustration as his accent grew thicker. "Yer twist my words, lass. I dinnae expect us to last long enough for yer to need to know."

"Yes, and I pressured you into more. But you're free. Please leave."

I closed my eyes and waited for his retreating footsteps. They didn't come.

"How many ways do I have to tell yer? It was too late the first time I saw yer. I had to have yer. I thought I could feck yer out of me mind, but I couldn't. I want more."

"It's too late. I can't trust you. Please just leave."

This time when I heard his steps, I blew out a breath and let the tears fall.

Though I couldn't say for sure what I felt for him, it hurt like hell knowing he was gone forever.

TWENTY-EIGHT

THE NEXT MORNING, LIZZY FOUND ME BURIED UNDER A mound of covers she removed.

"What happened?" she asked, concern written in the frown lines on her face.

"I'm stupid. That's what happened. Kalen's not only a cheat and a liar, he has a son."

Her eyes widened in surprise. "A child."

"Yes." Though it still surprised me, I told her the story from top to bottom.

When I was done, she sat in her best lawyer impression.

"Let me get this straight. He willingly took you home, a place where his nanny and son would be."

"Yes." I wasn't sure where she was going with this.

"Kalen doesn't seem stupid enough to bring you home where he'd be caught. Maybe he's telling the truth."

"About what? He certainly left out a big part of his life."

"Yes, but honey, you probably didn't grow up with a lot of single parents, especially ones everyone else didn't know."

I silently agreed.

"Well, think about it. What kind of father would he be if he introduces his son to every woman he sleeps with?"

"I didn't ask to meet him. But he should have told me."

Lizzy patted my shoulder. "And when was he supposed to do that? You admitted yourself that you guys hadn't become official until right before you were screwing him in his apartment. When did he have time exactly?"

I wanted to protest her logic, but she was right. I deflated.

"Don't beat yourself up. I would have drawn the same conclusions."

"What do I do now?" I pulled the covers over my head.

She pulled them away with a wide grin. "Give him a chance to sweat a little and make a move first. Then you will see if he's really committed."

I glanced over at my phone, which was plugged in but still turned off. I left it that way and only came out of my room when Lizzy coaxed me out. We watched a show about early twentieth-century Irish gangsters. The lead actor's blazing blue eyes only reminded me of Kalen's piercing green ones. Still, it passed the time.

My night ended with a Tylenol PM to help me sleep. I had to get back on track. Forget about men, or rather boys, and get my career back on track.

I woke up fresh, but still a little sad. I turned on my phone as I exited the elevator and noticed Kalen's driver standing in the lobby.

It wasn't a coincidence, but I kept walking by.

"Miss Glicks."

I let out the breath I'd been holding.

"If Kalen sent you, you can tell him I'm perfectly capable of riding the subway."

"As you will."

I exited the building, giving my confused doorman a little wave. As I walked, I had a feeling I was being followed and glanced over my shoulder. I came to a complete stop when I realized I was right.

"I told you, I'm fine," I said to Kalen's driver.

"I'm sure you are, miss. But I'm under strict orders to make sure you get safely to work."

I gave the man a smile. It wasn't his fault his boss was an ass.

"So, tell him you did."

"I will after you arrive."

I pointed at the SUV at the curb. "What about your car? It will be towed."

He shrugged. "I'll get it after you get to work."

I blew out a frustrated stream of frosted air and headed for the SUV. I wouldn't let him get in trouble for me. His boss and I would have words later.

In the back seat, a box with a bow waited for me. I glanced up and Kalen's driver nodded.

"Open it," he said.

Inside was a smart watch, not unlike the one Scott's fiancée wore to the holiday gala.

"I don't want his gifts," I said, knowing it would be reported back to his boss.

"It's for your safety, miss."

I let loose a bark of laughter. "He's got to be kidding."

"I'm afraid not."

"Let me guess. If you don't get it on my wrist, you'll be in trouble."

"Yes, miss."

I pulled out my phone and dialed the man in question.

"Miss Glicks."

Grrr. The infuriating man was back to Miss Glicks.

"I don't need your man servant to drive me to work," I chuffed as the driver chuckled.

"His name is Griffin."

Immediately, I felt terrible. "I'm sorry," I said to Griffin.

"No problem, miss."

"I don't need a driver," I revised.

"You mentioned a note yesterday and I assume it wasn't a friendly one. The only person I'm involved with is you. So who sent it?"

"Any exes?" I asked.

I wasn't certain I wanted that answer.

"No."

"Then it's probably Scott's fiancée," I reasoned.

"If I remember correctly, at the party, she mentioned not sending you a note either."

She had.

"Like she's going to be honest," I said.

"And what if she is? Then someone is targeting you? Why?"

I didn't have an answer. "Why the watch?" I asked.

"Because you can make a call on it even if you don't have your phone."

It was all reasonable. But I didn't like feeling afraid.

"You don't have to take care of me," I said.

"I don't. Let Griffin drive you to work."

"But the note was left on my door," I said, thinking out loud.

"Then he'll walk you there and check your apartment when he picks you up."

"Wait!" I said.

"I have a meeting. I'll talk to you later."

He was gone.

"Can you tell me where I'm driving you?" Griffin asked.

The man was in an impossible position I wouldn't make worse. I gave him the address to King Enterprises, and after following the quick-start instructions, I fitted my new watch around my wrist.

Good thing I hadn't told Kalen that I'd received the first note at work. It would have been impossible to get Griffin through security.

As soon as I walked into the conference room, I froze in place. My co-workers were staring at me like I was a newsflash.

"What's going on?" I asked hesitantly.

"Scott's in a mood," Jim said.

Anna nodded. "He mumbled something, then left in a huff."

"What does that have to do with me?" I asked innocently. But I knew exactly what Scott's problem was. I'd sent the email about my findings yesterday evening.

She shrugged. "He might have said your name."

I sat in my unofficial spot, opened my laptop, and grinned. I didn't get pleasure from hurting people, but Scott deserved whatever the partner-in-charge gave him for trying to take credit for my work.

The last of the bank confirmations had come through when Scott tore into the office.

"Can I speak to you?"

I didn't bother to check if he was talking to me. I got up and followed him back in the hall.

"You seem to have forgotten the chain of command," Scott said.

I could tell he'd been at a simmering boil for a while.

"Maybe if you hadn't tried to take credit for my work, I wouldn't have to overstep you."

"I'm the senior-in-charge," he said.

"Then act like it. Everyone knows a senior wouldn't be doing grunt work like confirming cash accounts unless the person underneath him wasn't doing their job. I won't let you ruin my reputation to climb your career ladder."

Red-faced, he stood there a second. "You don't understand how important this assignment is. I have a baby coming."

I let out a sardonic laugh. "Seriously. As I recall, you mentioned wanting to get a bonus so you could buy a watch. That's what you're after."

His thin lips flattened. "I don't even know if that's my kid. I was careful."

"I can't believe I ever thought I loved you." I shook my head. "You're all about avoiding responsibility and taking credit that's not yours."

He might have said something, but a flash of inky hair caught my attention. The tall frame was familiar, and I moved in that direction.

"Bailey," Scott called at my back, but I didn't stop.

By the time I made it to the end of the hall that inter-

sected with the elevator banks, the doors on one were closing. *It couldn't be*, I told myself.

"Bailey, what the hell?" I glanced up and Scott was
there. "Where were you going?"

"I thought—" I began, but stopped myself. Why was I
explaining myself to him? "It's nothing."

"You have a lot of work to do. I've spoken to the head of
the accounting department and he assures me that we will
have all the requested information by the end of the day. It
will be a late night. Don't think about leaving early."

He stalked off and I rolled my eyes, tempted to flip him
off while sticking out my tongue, but I resisted. Only
because this hallway was more frequently used, and I'd look
like a dumb teenager. The jerk knew how to push my
buttons.

I went back to the conference room, and as promised
the information I'd requested started coming in. By the time
I left, I was starving. I'd forgotten all about Griffin until I
walked outside to find him waiting.

He opened the door on the SUV like it was inevitable
that I'd accept the ride. Tired and frustrated, I slid into the
back without complaint. On the seat was a rectangular box
with a beautiful ribbon holding it together.

Griffin got in and nodded at me. "That's for you, miss."

I was done with the formality. "You can call me Bailey."

He nodded. "Fine, Bailey. Let's get you home."

Though I hated to see the perfectly made bow taken
apart, curiosity won. I lifted the top and inhaled deeply.
Laid neatly on a bed of tissue were several lacy bras and
matching underwear. There were even a couple of garters.
My cheeks heated as I almost pulled one out to look at it

until I remembered Griffin would be able to see me. I'd shut my eyes just long enough for Griffin to pull to a stop and say, "You're home, miss."

Upstairs, after I waved Griffin off, I wrangled the door open, managing my purse, tote, and the box without dropping anything. Lizzy was in the kitchen with a bottle of wine in her hand.

"What do you have there?" she asked.

I set the box on the island and the rest of my stuff on a barstool. Then with my eyes on hers, I lifted the lid.

Her eyes went a little unfocused as they did when she walked into her favorite store.

"You went shopping?" she said more than asked.

I shook my head. "No."

Her eyebrows shot up. "A gift from Mr. Hot Scot?"

"Why do you insist on calling him that?"

"Because he's hot and he's Scottish. It works. Go with it."

"More like gorgeous but grumpy," I grumbled to myself.

"Did he leave a note?" she asked, ignoring me.

I lifted the envelope, which was suspiciously like the cardstock used in the warning note, which worried me.

She took it from my hand. "Have you read it?"

"No," I said.

She held it out to me. "Read it."

Though I hated the fear that overtook me, I snagged it from her hand. As I pulled out the familiar thick paper, the note inside read, *I owed you one. K—.*

"Well," Lizzy prodded.

I turned the paper around so she could read it.

"My, my, my. What dirty deeds did he do in bed?" I

gave her a look that told her not to ask. "Fine. Are you going to keep them?"

"I don't know."

She lifted a bra out and sighed. "So pretty. There's like a couple grand of lingerie here." Appalled, I gaped. Lizzy laughed. "Not everyone gets their underwear from Target."

"It's functional."

"Exactly, and this will make your man beg."

"He's not my man," I protested.

She put the bra back before patting my hand. "Of course, he is. A man like him doesn't buy La Perla for anyone. It's too bad your boobs are bigger than mine. I'd take them off your hands."

"I can't accept this." I waved a hand over the box with too expensive underwear in it.

"It's too late to return it. He didn't leave you a gift receipt and the price tags have been removed."

"I'll donate them."

Shocked, she opened her mouth and stopped before speaking. "Honey, you don't donate La Perla. You go to Target, buy some functional underwear, and donate that if it makes you feel better. Besides, how many women in the world have your curves? This was bought specifically for you."

Though she seemed in awe, I was worried about his note. I took out a bra and looked at the tag. 34D. Perfect.

"How does he know my size?"

"He pays attention," she said gently like she knew I'd hate her answer.

I picked up the envelope, unable to get it out of my

217

mind and handed it to her. "How easy is it to get stationary like this?"

She inspected it. "I'd say pretty easy. It's expensive, but there's nothing truly unique about it. Why?"

When she gave it back, I studied the writing. The script was masculine and looked nothing like the handwritten warning notes. I tried to breathe easier.

"Bails, are you okay? You look a little pale."

I glanced up. "I'm fine. Just tired."

I tapped the note in my hand and worked to shake the idea that maybe Kalen was somehow involved in trying to put my audit findings to a stop. The fact that I swore I saw him in the office today didn't help.

In my room, I shot Kalen a text.

Me: I can't accept the gift.

Quicker than I thought, he responded.

K: It's yours to do with as you like.

Me: Can't you return it? It's too expensive.

K: Like I said in the note, I owed you.

Me: You broke only one.

K: Consider the rest interest.

Me: I can't wear underwear that costs more than the clothes covering them.

K: Then you need new clothes.

At first, I thought he was insulting me until I realized the trap I'd walked myself into.

Me: Do not buy me any clothes.

I waited for a reply in vain because nothing came. When I woke the next morning, Lizzy stood in my doorway with a huge tan box tied with a simple black ribbon.

"This came for you."

I rolled off the bed and stalked over to her. I snatched the box and tossed it onto the bed like it burned my hands.

"Look who's the grumpy one this morning," she muttered.

"He's an ass," I snapped.

"A rich one."

I spun to face her. "You can have him."

"He's not my type. Besides, I think he's more than a little hung up on you. Now, go ahead and open it. Take a girl out of her misery. I'm dying to know what he's bought you this time."

Unable to resist the allure of a mystery, which made me good at my job, I undid the binding and opened the lid.

As I stood there staring inside, Lizzy moved in. She slid the note to the side and picked up the first item.

"Oh my, an Alexander McQueen Fit & Flare Poplin Button-Front Blouse that bands at the waist and a peplum hem."

All of that went over my head. I saw a white, long-sleeved shirt that was functional yet too fashionable for me.

Lizzy was way too giddy as she set the blouse down like it could break and picked up something else.

"He's paired it with a Tom Ford off-center two-way exposed zip fitted pencil skirt. Sexy yet understated as you can adjust the front slit with the zip."

It was just a black skirt to me. Though I could imagine Kalen unzipping it off me and quickly pushed the thought out of my mind.

"Don't forget these." Lizzy held up a pair of black red-soled shoes. "Elegant yet classic Christian Louboutin Pigalle Plato Patent Red Sole Pump."

Overwhelmed, I asked, "How do you even know all of this?"

"I'm in art. It's my job to know fashion." She might as well have said "duh" for the look she gave me. "Or at least that's what I used to tell my mother when she'd get my credit card bill. Thank God I have control over my trust fund now."

"It's all yours," I said, heading to the bathroom to shower.

"No can do, my love," she called after me. "That man has plans and I'm not standing in the way of them."

I grumbled as I shut the door.

"You didn't read the note," I faintly heard through the closed door before I turned on my shower.

When I was finished, Lizzy was gone from my room. With the towel wrapped around me, I spotted the note and gave in to temptation. I sat down and read it.

Accessories for your lingerie. K—

After checking the sizes on the garments and shoes, I wondered again how he'd know the right ones. Dumbly, I hadn't asked in our text conversation. I'd been flustered. But I wasn't this morning.

I didn't dress in his offerings. I put on a white button-up shirt and simple black pencil skirt I'd gotten on sale at Ann Taylor. Then, I slipped on a pair of black Nine West pumps. Yet another sale item. I smiled a little as I left for work, knowing Griffin would be waiting for me. I hoped he reported to his boss that I wore a version of what he'd bought me that cost a fraction of what he'd probably spent.

Griffin was, in fact, there at the curb waiting to open the door for me. I'd agreed to the rides because Kalen had convinced me that maybe I was in danger. I was beginning to think the only person I was in danger from was Kalen himself.

But it was the folded piece of paper I found in my conference room chair that unnerved me.

TWENTY-NINE

A RED OCTAGON THAT TOOK UP MOST OF THE EIGHT-BY-ten sheet of paper glared up at me. Immediately, I looked around, the stop sign symbol an obvious warning. But the only people around were my co-workers.

"Did you guys see this?" I held it up for Kevin and Jim to see. Anna hadn't arrived yet. Both shook their heads as Scott walked in.

"What's that?" Scott asked.

I shifted so he could get a better look.

"I don't know. It was in my chair."

"It's just a paper. The cleaning people could have left it," Scott said.

Annoyed, I said more firmly, "But it was in my chair."

"It doesn't have your name on it or anything, does it?" Scott asked.

I grimaced and let the paper crumple in my fist because what could I do? Call the police and suggest that someone was threatening me with a stop sign? There was no writing to suggest this was directed at me, nor any hint of a repercussion. The cops would think I was crazy.

Instead, I got to work matching the information that King's accounting department provided for the weird wire transactions.

Just before lunch everything fell into place.

"Scott, come here, please."

Aggravation contorted his features as he said nothing in front of the team and stepped over.

"What is it?" he asked.

"See this." I pointed on my screen to the list I compiled. "They claim most of the wires are partner distributions from their private equity firm, but the wires I'm questioning aren't happening when the main distributions are made. They're either days before or days after. I think we should compare with the list of partners."

"I have that," Jim said. "I confirmed contributions and distributions. All of the latter happened on the same days."

"See," I said to Scott. "Something is going on here."

"Good job," Scott agreed, and stood straight as if he planned to walk away.

"What are we going to do?"

I made the mistake of grabbing his forearm. His smile warmed, but it made my skin crawl. I let go.

"We are going to do nothing. We aren't forensic accountants with the FBI or SEC, Bailey. I'll bring it to the partner's attention. We will include the finding in our opinion."

"That's it?" I asked, feeling my blood boil. "What if this is fraud? Shouldn't management be notified?"

"I'll handle it," Scott said with finality. "Anna is out with the flu. If you are finished, work on completing Anna's open items. We need to wrap this assignment up in the next day or two."

Through gritted teeth, I said, "Sure," as pleasantly as I could muster.

It felt wrong that management wouldn't be notified of fraud until our firm issued an opinion on the financial statements. The partner-in-charge would review everything. It was unlikely that would happen in a day.

It was possible my next move could mark me as a troublemaker. I sent an email directly to the partner regarding my findings. If I lost my job, I could always go home, but with my head held high. That could be the sign that I wasn't meant for the secular world.

I'd just walked outside at the end of the day when my name rang out. I turned and sidestepped pedestrians on the sidewalk to find Scott.

"Bailey," he said and cupped the side of my head.

Before I could stop what was happening, his lips were on mine. I took a giant step away from him, angling to better face him. It left me staring between him and the doors I'd just come through.

When Scott grinned, my heart sank. I turned and locked my gaze with Kalen's stormy one. I drifted on watery legs with the need to say something despite all that had happened between us.

"Kalen, I can explain," I said when I reached him.

He stood in tailored clothing like a man ready to conquer the world and used his fingertips to silence my lips. He shook his head and opened the door. Heart thudding in my chest, I got into the car without protest, knowing we could talk on the ride.

"Griffin, take Miss Glicks home," Kalen said, shutting the door, not getting in.

I watched in horror as Kalen stood, back to me, facing Scott, whose sardonic grin hadn't diminished. I tried in vain to open the door so I could stop what was about to happen, but it was locked. Then the car was moving away.

Multiple calls I placed went unanswered. I'd even tried Scott. Frustrated, I slammed the door after walking into my apartment. Lizzy wasn't home, as she hadn't come to see what the ruckus was about. I stripped down in my room and washed away my annoyance in the shower.

By the time I finished, I felt marginally better. I walked into my room and came to a stumbling stop. There, looming in my doorway like the Grim Reaper, was Kalen. A war brewed in his gaze as if he wasn't sure he wanted to be there.

"Kalen," I said, breathing hard from my racing heart.

"Don't talk," he said, his voice rough like he hadn't used it in hours.

The possibility of a dream was quickly dismissed, and I asked, "Why are you here?"

He closed the distance and brushed the wet strands of hair away from my face.

"When you didn't answer your phone, I was worried about you."

"How'd you get in?" I asked.

"I let myself in."

"I didn't give you a key," I said stupidly.

"I'm handy with a lock." His smirk was too self-assured.

"Lizzy let you in."

He shrugged, not answering one way or another. I would talk to Lizzy later and confirm things.

"I'm still mad at you," I said, unsure how truthful that statement was. Still, I gripped the towel firmly at my breasts to hold it there.

His thumb brushed over my mouth, more tenderly than his expression revealed. He looked beyond angry. "Are you now?"

I couldn't answer, not without lying at least partially. I went for another tactic, wanting to regain some of my composure. Though I'd asked the question before, his answer hadn't been the complete story. I repeated myself, "Why are you here?"

My wrists were suddenly captured in his hands as he walked me backward and planted them on either side of my head when my back met the wall. He leaned down and whispered over my lips, "My cock has waited too long to be buried inside you."

He gently bit my ear and skimmed his teeth down the line of my throat, eliciting a groan from me when I should have told him to go to hell.

Both of my wrists were pulled together in one of his big hands and lifted over my head.

"Tell me to stop."

My throat grew tight as I couldn't force the words from my mouth.

"Last chance," he said, taking hold of the towel, fingers brushing over the tops of my breasts.

I held his gaze as words couldn't express what I was feeling: excitement, anger, turned-on, and daring.

Seconds later, as we stood waiting for the other to make

a move, he tugged the towel free. It fell from my body, leaving me exposed.

He gingerly cupped my breast. Bringing the tip to a peak, he sucked it into his mouth.

I melted in his hold, but found the words that needed to be spoken.

"Your cock wants to be here. But what about you?"

His pants-covered knee wedged between my legs and spread them.

"It's up for debate."

His response sent signals to my brain that I should be insulted. But the T-junction of my thighs had other ideas as his free hand headed south like a runaway freight train, taking all my reason with it.

"Don't move," he demanded when I angled my hips to rub myself more on his hand and possibly reach the bulge that was in his pants. When he let go of my wrists, I almost reached out to touch him. Then I remembered his command for me not to move. I so didn't want him to stop, because I was already teetering on the edge.

When he reached up to loosen his tie, I recognized that he was still wearing the one he'd had on earlier. But I didn't expect him to bind my wrists.

"Why?" I asked.

"Because you don't deserve to touch me," he said, without humor.

"That goes both ways," I challenged.

He stilled and used his penetrating gaze to pin me in place. "Tell me to stop, Miss Glicks. That's your right."

The ass knew I wouldn't. "You're not going to call me lass?"

"You lost the right to be called lass when you let him kiss you." It wasn't a question; it was a statement. "It remains to be seen if you will ever be lass again."

I was reminded of how we got here.

"What did you do to Scott?" I asked, wondering how it might affect my job if Scott went crying to one of the partners, including his dad, that Kalen did anything to him.

"Why are we talking about him? If you want to use that pretty little mouth of yours, you can wrap it around my cock."

I might have replied if he hadn't roughly sucked my nipple into his mouth, only to tenderly lick and nip sweetly. I couldn't make heads or tails of his mood as he continued his assault on my breast, pinching one and sucking the other before gently biting, taking me to the edge and back before doing the same to the other.

He kissed his way down my body until he was on his knees before me, still sexy in his suit. I should have felt powerful, yet he held all the power as he parted my nether lips and licked a blazing trail from my nub to my hole. I choked back a cry and panted, wanting him to continue until I went over the edge.

As if he purposefully wanted to torture me, he removed his mouth. Seconds later, he stood, flipping me around so fast I'd barely caught my breath before he spread my legs.

"There's a perfectly good bed," I mentioned with my cheek pressed to the wall.

"And how did that go for us?"

My undoing began when I heard his zipper and felt the soft fabric of his clothes against my back. I didn't want to remember that night and didn't when the head of his cock pierced my opening. He inched his way in too slowly and I bucked my hips, needing him deeper.

"You're so bloody tight," he said, taking his time, inch by inch.

When his balls slapped my ass and the tip of his dick hit the end of me, he leaned over my shoulder and picked a hell of a time to want to talk. I squirmed and caught sight of his pants hanging on to his thighs for dear life. It only turned me on more to know he wanted me so bad, he couldn't waste time with taking off his clothes.

"Do you still love your fiancé?"

I shook my head. "No," I whimpered as he pulled out a little.

"Do you want him back?"

Again, I shook my head until he kissed the nape of my neck and I wiggled my ass.

"Stop moving," he said, swatting me lightly on the side of my bottom. "Yet, you let him kiss you."

"He kissed me, and I pushed him away."

I sucked in air when he thrust in deep again and pulled almost all the way out.

"One more question. What about Matt, Lizzy's brother? Have you fucked him?"

Because there was anger in his voice, I didn't say I thought we covered this ground. I just answered. "Never."

He slammed his big cock in me and said, "Good."

As he found a rhythm, he grasped my hair and tugged a little as he assaulted my neck with kisses that sent shivers down my spine. He made his way up to my ear and spoke very clearly. "When you wrapped your lips around my cock, they became mine. You're mine, Miss Glicks. Tha thu a 'mhèinn. Do we understand each other?"

"Yes," I breathed.

"Say it," he demanded.

"I'm yours," I said right before he rammed into me again and again, building my orgasm with each penetrating stroke. He let go of my hair and gripped my hips, shifting himself to stroke over my G-spot with every thrust. It almost became too much as I moaned out my pleasure.

"When you come, you're going to forget any man came before me."

And like that, I came apart bit by bit, stifling a scream. His breaths at my ear became more erratic as he followed me to the sweetest ecstasy I'd ever experienced.

As I sagged against the wall, I was lifted in the cradle of Kalen's arms but not for long. He set me gently on the bed, my eyelids fluttering shut. I heard him in the bathroom, running water. Soon after, he was there cleaning me up.

"Sleep, lass."

I gave in to the pull and woke up alone. I sat up, about to call out Kalen's name, but I found him, suit and hair sexily rumbled, sitting in the armchair across from my bed.

"You didn't leave."

"I didnae."

He was back to his native tongue, which could only mean one thing. That he was at war with himself.

"Your son," I said, checking the time.

It was a little after eight. Had he missed dinner with his son?

"I want you to meet him."

THIRTY

KALEN WANTED ME TO MEET HIS SON. THAT HAD TO BE a huge deal on his part. I scooted back so my back leaned on the wall. "You do?"

"You've turned my world inside out. I can't close my eyes without seeing your face. I don't have a free moment when I'm not thinking about you. My dick is a loyal son of a bitch and only has eyes for you." He paused as he got close. "You weren't supposed to matter. No woman ever has. Yet I can't let you walk away." Air felt heavy in my chest. "Tell me, lass. Do you want to meet him?"

It was a question I hadn't given much thought to because I'd assumed things were over between us. Now with his declaration hanging between us, I was tongue-tied. It wasn't like I was afraid of loving a man with a child. I grew up where everyone in the community was family, blood or not. The question was, if I loved this man?

"Are you sure?" I asked, evading the question.

No matter what he said, he'd made it clear how important his son was to him. I agreed with his position on not introducing his son to women with whom he had a sexual relationship who ultimately didn't matter. Was he telling me that I mattered?

"Tomorrow night, seven."

I thought about the audit and how Scott said we had to wrap it up.

"I can't." His brow rose and I revised my answer. "It's work. I'll probably have to stay late."

"Problems?" he asked.

"I really shouldn't talk about it," I said, thinking about all the rules that governed my chosen career.

"Then don't." He moved forward, resting his arm on his leg. "But it looks as though you need to get something off your chest."

Was I that transparent? Truth was, I wanted to talk it through with someone who would understand. Kalen was a businessman and probably understood numbers better than Lizzy. If I talked about it in broad strokes without revealing who the client was, I should still be within the bounds of my contract and accounting rules.

"It's just, I found something, and no one wants to do anything about it. It feels wrong to say nothing to the client," I admitted.

"Tell someone," he offered.

"I would, but the people I'm in contact with most likely have something to do with it or they're colluding with someone else."

"How bad is it?"

"Really bad."

"Do you think the notes have anything to do with it?"

"Maybe," I said reluctantly. I wanted to believe it was a jealous woman because of the handwriting.

Though I wasn't one hundred percent sold on that. What would someone gain by bullying me? I was small potatoes. Besides, I'd already asked the questions. What more could I do? My thoughts trailed off as Kalen spoke.

"Then it's a good thing Griffin's driving you to work."

Ideas whirled in my head, competing with one another. I spun my legs over the side of the bed and stood, speaking my thoughts out loud and pacing. "What if it is someone in that department? They've heard my questions and they aren't bothered by them because they've covered their trail. Yet, they don't want me to escalate it to a higher level."

I lifted my eyes to Kalen's.

"Who are your suspects?"

I didn't think when I answered about what lines I was crossing.

"The lady in charge of the department I'm working with and/or her minion." The little weasel who seemed irritated by my questions.

"Anyone else?"

Scott came to mind, but I didn't say it. He was far too nonchalant about my findings. But that would mean he was working with someone on the inside. Then again, he had found a way on this audit. It was possible he'd wanted to be there, and not the excuse he'd given me.

"Maybe," I mused.

"Who?" he asked.

I smiled, enjoying that he was interested in my work. Though I couldn't tell him everything. Saying this much out loud made me surer that I had to do something.

"There is someone else." *The Money Man.* The name on the account that the money had gone into was Money Man LTD as if he was rubbing the flagrant misuse of funds in our faces. Scott had ignored that information as well. It only added to him being a suspect.

The request to send the money had been authorized by Jeremy King, according to the information I'd combed through. However, that wasn't unusual, considering the wire was being passed off as a distribution. All the distributions were signed off by him.

When I met Kalen's inquiring eyes, I said, "Someone closer to the top." I pushed my hair back. "I don't know what to do."

Kalen got to his feet. "Tell someone."

It was my turn to say, "Who?"

"Go as far up as you can."

I raked my nails over my scalp until Kalen caught my hands and pulled them away from my head. "What if it's coming from the top?"

His hands, still holding mine between us, squeezed reassuringly.

"Then you've lost nothing. They probably already know you know."

I continued his line of thought. "And if they aren't involved, I'm alerting them to something that should be taken care of."

He nodded and brought my palms to his lips. He kissed each one.

"I have to go," he said, letting go of me.

We'd come so far, but there was still more ground to cover when it came to us.

Before he reached the door, I let loose from my tongue the words I'd held close for far too long.

"You're not going to kiss me."

The moment that followed seemed to hang there as if deciding to take the leap off a cliff.

"If I kiss you, I'll never leave."

Then he was gone, and I berated myself for not phrasing the question better. I still didn't have the answer I wanted. I still didn't know what that meant for us.

Yet tomorrow I was supposed to meet his son.

THIRTY-ONE

THE BOX OF CLOTHES KALEN HAD GIVEN ME SAT propped in the chair he'd vacated last night. I didn't remember him putting it there. Yet I hadn't been looking at the chair when he left. Was it a sign?

If I took Kalen's advice, wouldn't it be better to confront the CEO or his son in a power outfit?

I dressed for success, including the heels he'd gotten me, feeling better about the coming day than I had been for a very long time.

"You're wearing it," Lizzy squealed, up unusually early for her.

"I am." I couldn't help smiling back at her. "By the way," I said on my way out the door. "I'll be late coming home tonight."

"The weather people are predicting a major winter storm tonight. You might get snowed in."

I bit the corner of my lip. I wouldn't mind spending the night with Kalen. Though I wasn't sure if that was wise the first time meeting his son.

I smiled and winked at her, debating the prospect. "Maybe," I said.

She let out a barrage of questions that were muffled when the door closed between us.

Even the chill in the air couldn't stop the sunshine that lit my path. I glanced at the gray sky and wondered what Kalen would say if we were snowed in. I smiled at Griffin, who cheekily gave me a grin back.

It felt like nothing could go wrong since I had a plan. In fact, I planned on checking out the hobby store next to the building during lunch. I hoped they had something I needed.

When I walked in, Scott was standing by the door.

"You look nice today," he said, with no hint of anger at my rebuff.

Nor did he look any worse for wear. Kalen must not have confronted him.

"Thanks," I said and went to my seat.

I worked like the devil was chasing me, hoping to finish at a decent hour. My lunch was a sandwich I picked up from the coffee shop after making a quick shopping trip. By late afternoon, I was ready.

On my way back, Scott caught me in the hall.

"I wanted you to know I got the partner to agree to speak with upper management."

Relief felt good. "That's great. When do we meet with them?"

He sighed. "We aren't meeting them. Raymond and I have a meeting with them in less than ten minutes."

Since when did he get on a first name basis with one of the partners of our firm? Then again, his father was a partner. It was likely there had been tons of get-togethers between families.

"I want to be there," I said. My coat and bag felt like unnecessary weight when I was about to fight for my career. "It's my report."

He sighed. "How about this?" He dug into his pocket and pulled out something he put in my hand.

I opened it to find the ring. The one I'd worn before Melissa had, and now he was giving it back to me. I looked up in horror.

"Before you speak. This is a good thing. You and I make an excellent team. We were also great together as a couple," he said.

Astonishment at his gall didn't cover what I was feeling. "She's pregnant."

"And not with my kid. She's gone. You can move in," he said as if that made everything between us good.

"How could you possibly know?"

Of course, there were DNA tests. But why would he do that? Then again, maybe his mother had suggested it.

"She admitted to it."

"What?" My gaze widened and my mouth hung open.

"She was jealous of you, and during our fight, she admitted that I wasn't the father."

Somehow, I didn't believe him. "Then who is?"

It wasn't really the time, but maybe placating him would get him to agree to let me in on the meeting.

"It's my father's." He could have sprouted devil horns and I would have been less surprised. "What do you say?"

He was far too cheery for a man who learned his girlfriend was screwing not only him, but his father too.

"I can't," I said.

I wanted to say something like, *never in a billion years, even if the planet needed repopulating*, but that would kill any chances of me going with him to the meeting.

"Why? For that Kalen guy. He's a fraud, you know."

I narrowed my eyes. "You don't know him."

"Precisely. And neither do you. Mother checked her circles, and no one has heard of a Kalen Brinner."

"She doesn't know everyone. This is New York."

His mother only wished she had the status Lizzy's parents did.

"The man wore a half-million-dollar watch. That kind of money means he would be known."

He reached for my cheek, but I moved out of reach.

"Don't be stupid, Bailey. He's a pretender, who is using you."

"For what?" I snapped. "I have nothing."

I wasn't going to mention that I wore thousands of dollars' worth of shoes and clothes Kalen had given me.

"Yes. And isn't it interesting he shows up while you're assigned to an audit to find out if the illustrious King Enterprises private equity firm is being accused of the biggest scandal since Bernie Madoff."

I took an involuntary step back as if I'd been slapped.

"You're putting it together. Not so smug, are you? You should consider my offer. It expires when the day is over," he said.

He turned and headed for the elevator. I didn't like where my head was going. A glance at the wall of windows and I caught my co-workers dipping their heads as if they hadn't been watching our show.

A moment too late, I ran after Scott, still wearing my coat and carrying my package. The elevator doors had just closed when I rounded the corner.

I tapped the button several times until one opened for me. I chose the top floor and prayed that was where the CEO's offices were.

When I reached the top, I caught sight of Scott heading for a conference room a little to the left and behind the receptionist's desk. I followed after him.

"Miss," a woman called out.

I ignored her. "Wait," I said, catching Scott's attention.

He turned, and that's when I spotted the tall, dark-haired form I would know anywhere.

"What? You shouldn't be here," Scott said.

Despite everything he'd told me, I couldn't give up on Kalen. There had to be an explanation.

"Maybe I was wrong?" I said, defending the man despite my growing suspicions. "We should take some more time examining the information."

Scott chuffed. "It's all here, Bailey."

"Scott."

We looked over to find the partner waving us in. The problem was everyone in the room turned our way.

I might have run, unable to watch as my findings were used to destroy the man I was falling desperately for. But when Kalen's face didn't register shock, everything inside me broke.

Scott looked back at me as if putting it all together. Of course, my little plea at the end didn't look good. I'd made myself look guilty as hell.

243

My ex chuckled darkly as he strode into the conference room like he owned it.

When our boss just stood in the doorway waiting, I walked in just as Scott dropped the bomb.

"You threaten me while you've been screwing her so she would accept these fraudulent wires you approved as legitimate."

Scott had spoken to Kalen, but there were others in the room. A very attractive older man who vaguely resembled Kalen and another man. He was younger than Kalen and also bore some resemblance.

"Bro, I was joking when I said screw one of the auditors."

"Quiet, Connor," the older man said.

I kept my eyes down, certain all eyes were on me.

"Did you know he was a King?"

As much as I didn't want to, I met my boss' eyes and answered his question. "No. He told me his name was Kalen Brinner."

"That's true," Scott said.

"His name is Jeremy King," the eldest King said.

I closed my eyes, afraid he would say that after he'd called the other guy Connor. I opened them when Kalen corrected him by saying, "Jeremy Kalen Brinner King."

If he thought that mattered, he was wrong. I felt betrayed, used, and mostly stupid. Once again, a man had thoroughly played me for the idiot I was.

"Clear the room," Mr. King said.

As Scott passed me, I turned to follow him out.

"Not you, young lady."

My boss interjected, "We will deal with our own."

"I have questions for her," the older man declared.

They both looked at me. "As long as it has nothing to do with the audit," my boss said.

Mr. King waved him off, leaving me alone in the hot seat.

After the door closed, Mr. King turned on his oldest son.

"When did you know she was a part of the auditing team?"

I shifted to look at the man who'd torched my faith in men to ash. He put a finger in his collar as if to loosen it. Then his eyes found mine and he spoke as if only to me.

"I spotted our corporate lawyer at her firm's holiday party. He wouldn't tell me why he was there, but she mentioned the party included clients."

The older man cleared his throat and caught my attention. "And he never once told you who he was? You never guessed?"

"She didn't know," Kalen said, his jaw tight.

"I didn't," I said, defending myself.

Mr. King stared at me, and I stood there back straight.

"She's pretty, Jeremy, but you know better—"

"May I be excused?" I asked, falling back on how I'd been brought up to be respectful to my elders no matter what. And I wouldn't have been able to do that if I stayed there and let him insult me.

He pointed at me. "I like that she has manners." Though he'd been looking in my direction, he hadn't spoken to me. "Yes, you may leave."

I hustled out of the room, only to be greeted by Scott and our boss, who ended a phone call when he spotted me.

"Miss Glicks, I'm sure this comes as no surprise that you can no longer work on this assignment. Additionally, you will be on administrative leave until a full review can be done to see how far you compromised this audit."

A scream of frustration and anger wanted out more than words, so I nodded and held it in. When the door opened, and the younger King waved my boss in, I walked with as much dignity as I could in the opposite direction.

I didn't make it halfway there when an arm hooked around mine to stop me.

THIRTY-TWO

KALEN

THERE WAS A MOMENT WHEN I THOUGHT I WOULD KILL my father. I'd already moved and stood right in front of the man.

"Dinnae talk about her like that or I'll cut off your tongue and shove it down your gullet."

The old man didn't back down and only waved me off.

"I can't understand you when you get like this. Speak English, son. Are you upset I called your pretty auditor a whore?"

Connor was there, which probably saved my father's life. He held the arm that I'd been about to swing with.

"I warned yer. I won't say it again. And don't call me son. You haven't earned that right."

The old man laughed. "Don't be a fool. That woman will only bring you grief. Take it from me. I loved your mother, gave her the world, and she left me."

I shook off my brother. "Because you brought her here where she knew no one and left her on her own, only to screw around on her."

He spread his arms. "I was building an empire for her, us. She tightened those legs of hers, and what was I supposed to do?"

I barreled toward the man who helped give me life, ready to take his. Connor, though slightly smaller than me, bear hugged me before I made good on my threats.

"You're walking a tight rope, son. Those auditors have found something. If you've been working against me, I will make sure not only your life, but your mother's is hell. And when you're rotting in prison, my grandson will follow in my footsteps."

"Calm down, big guy," Connor said in my ear. "He's not worth it. Think of Gabe."

Hearing my son's name was the only thing that calmed me.

"Let me go," I demanded.

Connor did and went to the door.

Before he opened it, I said, "I'm only here because you're a dying old man. Remember that."

I wanted to punch a hole in the wall, but it was glass. When I passed the dobber Bailey had called fiancé, the little arsehole smirked at me. It didn't matter. I needed to find my woman before she left thinking the worst of me.

She was heading to the elevator when I caught her.

"Wait. We need to talk."

The fire that I loved that matched her hair rose and stiffened her spine.

She eyed the place where I held on to her and I let go. Then her narrowed eyes steadied blankly on mine.

"We. Don't. Need. To. Talk. About. Anything. I've heard enough."

"You haven't heard everything." When she angled her head like we should have it out right there in the open, I said, "Five minutes."

She glanced at the watch I'd given her. "Counting."

"Not here. Follow me."

She wasn't going to let me touch her, so I put my hand at the small of her back to guide her to my office.

We were stopped short by the very lawyer I spoke with at her holiday party.

"This isn't advisable," he said, his gaze bouncing between us.

"I need to speak with her."

"Jeremy, I must caution against this. You and she cannot have any more contact."

When had my father notified him?

"I need five minutes."

I didn't wait for him to approve and ushered her into my office, closing the door on my father's right-hand man. She stopped and turned to face me, owning me in that moment.

There was so much I needed to say. So much more she needed to know. I was stopped short when she started clapping.

THIRTY-THREE

BAILEY

"Congratulations. You had me completely fooled, but that's what I am. A fool, isn't it?"

"Lass."

I jabbed a finger in his direction. "Somehow, I don't think legally you can call me that anymore. Why don't we go back to Miss Glicks? That's how you saw me anyway."

He prowled forward. I lifted the arm with all my bags in front of me as some sort of shield. "Don't touch me," I warned.

His hands rose in a position of submission. "Let me explain."

"No. You're always explaining." I used my free hand to wipe a tear at the corner of my eye. "You have so many secrets I can't keep up. But the truth is, when I thought you were listening to me last night, you were prodding me for information."

"It's not like that," he said, moving to erase some of the distance between us.

"Sure, it is. I let myself fall for you against my better

judgment, and all I was to you was a game you played and won. You claimed my heart like some sort of trophy. And I let it happen. Stupid me."

My eyes fell to my ring. Would I forever be paying for my sins against the one man who had truly loved me? The one man I fully trusted. And not the man who stood before me.

"You're not stupid. I am. I should have told you the truth. But I couldn't let you go. And if you knew, you would have walked away."

I nodded, even though he hadn't asked a question.

"That's why I kept it to myself." He hesitated before adding, "I'm falling in love with you."

I choked out a laugh and covered my mouth as it changed to a sob as something broke inside me. How many times had Scott profess his love to me, all the while cheating on me?

"How dare you say that? I don't even know who you are, *Jeremy*." Tears spilled freely from my eyes as I choked out the rest. "Your secrets have cost me my job."

"I'll fix it."

I shook my head. "You've done enough."

Then I lifted my chin. "Goodbye, Mr. King," I said formally, as a part of my heart died knowing we wouldn't ever see each other again.

He moved quicker than I could, capturing my face in his big hands. "We can make this work," he said.

I wanted to believe him and the desperate way he'd spoken. But I knew better.

"Believe me, it's just your dick that will miss me, if that. I'm sure there is a line of women willing to take my place."

"There's no one but you."

For a second, my resolve slipped. "You have a funny way of showing it. If you take a moment, you'll realize you've never once kissed me."

He traded a wide-eyed stare for my glare. Then his soft, yet urgent, mouth crashed against mine. In a weak moment, I gave in, letting his tongue stroke over mine as I deepened the kiss. In the back of my head, sense screamed at me to wake up. Desperately, I hung on for another minute before I pulled away.

"It's too late," I said, as my heart burned to dust. I pulled the gift I'd dipped into my savings to buy. "This is for your son."

I put the box with the Mercedes Vison model car that matched his perfectly in his hand and left him standing there. I thought it had been a sign of good fortune that I happened upon it over my lunch break in the hobby shop. How wrong I'd been.

As I made my way to the elevator, I made plans. I couldn't stay in New York. With a storm coming, I couldn't imagine sleeping in my room on a night I was supposed to meet his son and look at the walls he'd made love to me on.

When I stepped outside, the first of many snowflakes had started to fall. I gave Griffin the courtesy of a final conversation.

"Your job is done," I said, keeping my anger in check.

"It's not that easy, miss."

"Of course, it is. If you follow me, I will call the police and tell them you're stalking me."

Checkmate. Though I wasn't sure if I'd follow through

TERRI E. LAINE

with the threat. He begrudgingly gave me a smile and a tip of his head.

I took the subway home. When I got there, I packed a small bag. I wouldn't need much where I was going.

Four hours later, in my ice-covered rental car, I pulled up to the security gate.

"Bailey, long time no see," a guy I grew up with said. "It's really coming down."

"Hi, Samuel. It is. The drive was dicey, but I'm here."

"Go on ahead," he said, raising the gate.

Women's roles were far from progressive here. Old traditions and very old-fashioned values meant the jeans I wore wouldn't be allowed.

I parked in the snow-covered lot for visitors. Curiosity about the Amish had brought reporters and other people to our door, even though we weren't Amish. A small visitors center had been constructed for those allowed in where they would be required to drop off any electronics such as cell phones.

There wasn't anyone manning the small building, as no one had been expected. But I'd worked the job before. I tried Lizzy's phone again because it would be the last time I could call her, but she didn't answer. I'd left her a long and tearful message before I left, and so I simply hung up.

I logged in my things and locked them up. Then I went into the bathroom to change into the dress I'd taken with me when I left. It covered me from neck to feet, but it wasn't for cold weather. I was forced to wear my coat, which wasn't approved, as it hadn't been made by hand. But I didn't have another with me and needed it for the walk home.

The crunch of the snow underfoot in the silence only

heightened my nerves. I wasn't sure how I'd be received, especially by my father.

I walked the rest of the way to my parents' door and stopped short when I spotted a man working on our front window. His frame was too familiar.

He'd heard my approach and turned. It was as if time had stood frozen. He hadn't changed a bit. He was every bit as handsome as the last time I'd seen him. "Turner."

"Bailey," he said.

And my heart stopped as the sole ring I wore burned on my finger.

<<<<>>>>

I'd like to thank you for taking the time to read my novel. Above all, I hope you loved it. If you did, I would love it *if you could spare just a few minutes to leave a review ~ just a few words are fine.* I would greatly appreciate it. Thanks so much!

PART TWO OF THE KING MAKER SERIES
QUEEN OF MEN
IS AVAILABLE NOW.

USA TODAY BESTSELLING AUTHOR
TERRI E. LAINE

ACKNOWLEDGMENTS

Writing is not a right as much as it is a privilege. I wouldn't have that opportunity to do this if not for my readers. And I've been doing this now for a decade now, and I'm grateful for all the support my readers have shown me over the years. So THANK YOU.

Writing is also solitary at times. I'm alone with my thoughts and words, but nothing I put down on paper could be perfect if not for a solid team of beta readers behind me. They are first look that everything I think I got on the page actually made it there. So THANK YOU:

Kelly Reed-Brunet— I will never forgot the first time we met. You have been there for me in ways I can't even explain. Though you've been my cheerleader, I'd like to think of you as more than that. As a friend! xo

Diane Plourde— You are always there with a helping hand without any expectations to receive anything in return. I appreciate you so much. You are a treasure.

Tracy Lawson— You are fantastic. Thank you for reading and helping to make sure my Scottish hero didn't sound like he came out of a historical romance novel. And don't mind Amy. I never had problems understanding that amazing Scottish accent of yours.

Sue Bee—Thanks for reading the beginning and helping me make my alpha sound more alpha than beta.

Never to be forgotten – my writing partner Anne Hargrove. You are always there to help no matter what in my time of need. You are not only a great friend, but a bestie.

Amy Jennings—Thank you for helping me to see the world. If not for you, I my dreams of seeing Paris and Scotland would have never happened. But we didn't stop there. Never let the adventures end. I'm grateful for our friendship, bestie.

Thanks to Michele @ Michele Catalano Creative, one of the best designers out there. She always sees my vision even before I know it. Thank you for designing a beautiful cover.

To Sara, I may have bought this picture years ago; but saving it turned out to be the best thing. It just works here.

Thank you to Paige Smith. You are always there last minute to work me in. You give shine to my words.

A final thank you to Rosa Sharon at iScream Proofreading Services for your keen eye and extremely fast turnaround.

stalk
terri e. laine

ABOUT THE AUTHOR

Terri E. Laine, USA Today bestselling author, left a lucrative career as a CPA to pursue her love for writing. Outside of her roles as a wife and mother of three, she's always been a dreamer and as such became an avid reader at a young age.

Many years later, she got a crazy idea to write a novel and set out to try to publish it. With over a dozen titles published under various pen names, the rest is history. Her journey has been a blessing, and a dream realized. She looks forward to many more memories to come.

STALK ME AT

Website: terrielaine.com
Facebook: terrielainebooks
Facebook Page: TerriELaineAuthor
TikTok - @terrielaineauthor
Instagram @terrielaineauthor
Goodreads: terri e laine
Twitter: @TerriLaineBooks
Newsletter Signup:
https://www.subscribepage.com/terrielaine

Join my fan group
Terri's Butterflies or Terri's Badass Readers Group on
Facebook.

*I have several upcoming releases, make sure to sign up for
my newsletter or check my website for details.*
www.terrielaine.com

ALSO BY TERRI E. LAINE

other books co-authored

by Terri E. Laine